NO PLACE LIKE HOME

SHORT STORIES FROM THE LANDING

BY
MIKE R HUNTER

Independently published.
Copyright 2022, Mike R. Hunter

Cover photo and layout: Mike R. Hunter
Back cover: UFaux – West Bay, by J.M.B. Hunter
Bald Eagle: Shutterstock.

ISBN 978-1-7780695-1-2 (print)
978-1-7780695-0-5 (e-pub)

A copy of this book has been deposited with Library and Archives Canada Legal Deposit.

Facebook: Mike R Hunter
http://mike-r-hunter.blogspot.ca

No Place Like Home:
Short Stories From The Landing

No Place Like Home

Table of Contents

FEIGNED PRAISE
FOR STORIES FROM THE LANDING

"Too funny." B.S.

"Smart and funny, but more puns next time." J.S.C.

"So outrageous they could be true!" M.T. ('Not,' ed.)

"Amusing, I guess. Could do with fewer puns." P.P.

"Encore! Encore!" P.H. ('Thanks Mom,' ed.)

"Great sense of local history, rural life, timing and humour. Not as good as Frank Macdonald, but pretty good." F.M.

"Pull the other one!" Monty Python

"Can't wait for a follow-up!" Anon. (Let's see how this one goes, ed.)

FOREWORD

"[H]e told the truth, mainly. There was things which he stretched, but mainly he told the truth. That is nothing. I never seen anybody but lied one time or another...." *Introduction to The Adventures of Huckleberry Finn, by* Mark Twain

Taking his cue from Huck Finn, sort of, Mike Hunter says these stories are nothing *but* stretchers. Well, yes and no. The stories are works of fiction – pure bull, but triggered by a real event or some little thing he overheard said, from which his imagination and peculiar sense of humour took off all on their own, in the way stories sometimes do. He's no Mark Twain, but the stories are rather funny, if I do say so.

Mike invented the village of The Landing because he took so many liberties with the history, the buildings, geography and the people at the west end of Bras d'Or Lake where he lives. Most of the other places and geographical names are real, but here and there they've been moved around to benefit the tale. They say that truth is stranger than fiction, but fiction can be funnier than truth. You *can* make this stuff up!

Likewise, some stories are inspired by real people, but in an unreal way. Some are what they call composite characters, where the author takes this or that characteristic and blends it with someone else's – like the way Picasso pulled apart his subjects and put them back together in unusual ways, though I don't think Picasso meant to be humorous. Mike Hunter is no Picasso either. Some stories use the real name of real people or institutions just to mess with readers, but he intends no offence to anyone.

He's not too preachy either – the stories are meant to entertain, not teach. You can go to bed satisfied with having read a good yarn, without lying awake pondering some unresolved dilemma or wondering what happened next. The beauty of short fiction is that not every story has to have a beginning, middle and conclusion. The stories are not chronological, so you can read them in any order.

Point-of-view is not consistent either, which will annoy some critics and anyone trying to read reality into a story, or because they think they might recognize someone. The stories are mostly told by me (your omniscient narrator), except where it's first person of course, even though I only know what's written and even though I don't have a science background – such is the beauty of words.

Anyway, Huckleberry Finn said his was "mostly a true book, with some stretchers," but *Stories From The Landing* are nothing *but* stretchers.

Enjoy

Signed, Ed.

p.s. Mike knows that his kind of stories are of little interest to conventional publishers so, with apologies to former colleagues in that business, he's gone ahead and done this himself. He's not getting any younger.

FINDING AONGHAS

'Police in Port Hawkesbury are investigating a possible drowning, after an overturned boat was spotted off Marble Mountain late Thursday. Stay tuned to 101.5 The Hawk for news updates on the hour and on line at 1015thehawk.com. That's 1015thehawk.com.'

That's the sort of news that tends to shake a maritime community like The Landing – calling some folks to action out of a sense of duty, and everyone else to their windows out of curiosity. On such occasions Loch Bras d'Or seems to lap the shore at The Landing a little more savagely, and the whole village lists a degree or two as everyone moves at once to the water side of their respective houses.

Though the sea is in their blood, few people hereabouts actually depend on the loch for their livelihood, as had their ancestors. These days, every craft plying the turbulent surface of the loch is for pleasure; still, when watery tragedy strikes, all feel affected.

'The boat was recovered by the West Bay Road fire department's water rescue team, but as yet there is no official report of any occupants. Stay tuned to 101.5 The Hawk or 1015thehawk.com for updates.'

Facebook may be the grapevine for tens of millions of people everywhere else in the world, but in an area without mobile phone reception or reliable internet service, the local post office is still the source for news updates. That's where people learned that the recovered boat belonged to Aonghas Fleming from Marble Mountain. Aonghas was a seventy-something widower who stayed in a modest lochside house within sight of the road but distant enough to allow the privacy his ancestors sought nearly two centuries before.

Evidence mounted as the hours passed. It was Aonghas's boat alright. And there had been no lights in the house the night before and no smoke from the chimney in the morning. The car was in the yard, but that's where it most always was; he hardly went anywhere except to town for supplies, to the post office for his mail or to the hall for weekly coffee.

On Friday, the wind came up, and with it the rain as a nor'easter gathered strength along the shoreline from The Landing to Orangedale.

'RCMP have confirmed receiving a report of a body on the beach of MacRae's Island, about a kilometre off shore. Strong winds have rendered recovery impossible for the moment. For the latest news, weather and sports, stay tuned to 101.5 The Hawk or 1015thehawk.com. Follow us on Facebook at 1015thehawk.'

Enid MacLean, of upper Marble Mountain, reported seeing the body through binoculars from her front room before the weather obscured everything normally surveyed from her vantage point. That must have been frustrating. Enid took seriously her responsibility to keep everyone informed about everyone else's business.

By noon Saturday the wind had hauled around a bit and the weather and water calmed enough for a couple of boats to venture out – but no body was found. Arrangements were made for a dive team to return that afternoon or the next morning, depending on the forecast, but that effort was aborted at the last minute, and the team waited for further instructions.

'Another possible sighting this morning of a body in the water – the third such sighting in as many days. RCMP will not speculate whether or not they are connected. Stay tuned to 101.5 The Hawk for all the latest news.'

If police weren't speculating, Clennie MacLennan was. "What if it's not the same body?" he asked no one in particular outside church after services Sunday morning. The connection – three sightings, three days, in a pattern consistent with a nor'easter – was obvious, a no-brainer to everyone except Clennie. Aonghas Fleming was drowned.

But Clennie was having none of that. "They're not telling us everything – just the minimum. They don't want us to know. It could be a drug war."

"Cheezuss, Clennie," intoned Ant'ny White. "It's Aonghas. He's not home. No one's seen him for days. They found his boat. I heard the body was wearing those coveralls he got when he worked for the railway. It's Aonghas, and we better face up to it."

"Well, I don't believe it, and neither should you. It's the Americans. I told you there'd be trouble, and this is just the beginning."

∞∞

Monday morning at the post office offered no new news. Police called in search-and-rescue, and various

3

fire departments raced importantly but pointlessly up and down the worn-out road between The Landing and Marble Mountain.

Aonghas Fleming's neighbours became increasingly anxious and were helping police make sense of the clues and the geography. Dusk forced all to abandon their search until Tuesday morning.

'Port Hawkesbury RCMP have called for additional volunteers to search for clues, as the disappearance of a local man reported missing by neighbours and family continues to be investigated. Snow and colder temperatures are forecast for later Wednesday and officials fear it will further hamper their efforts. For the latest news, weather and sports, stay tuned to 101.5 The Hawk or 1015thehawk.com. Follow us on Twitter @1015thehawk.'

The resulting scour of the shoreline in the areas between the three sightings turned up additional clues as hoped: a Toronto Maple Leafs toque, a life jacket and a white rubber boot with a hole in it. The toque and life jacket had markings identifying them as Aonghas Fleming's. The boot, however, was much too small to have been his – what's more, according to the label it was a woman's.

Despite the boot, the clues solidified in people's minds Aonghas's fate and, just as assuredly, solidified Clennie's assertion that it was a multiple murder. The fact that the three different sightings could not be definitely connected of course elicited official-speak on the part of the RCMP and media.

'Police have declined to say whether they are dealing with a single incident or multiple. Your source for the

*latest news and community announcements is on line at
www.1015thehawk.com, that's www.1015thehawk.com.'*

By 1 p.m. Tuesday, everything that floats was being
deployed in an all-out effort to find Aonghas Fleming
before the weather turned again.

"Fake news," asserted Clennie, holding court in
the Tanneries Tavern. "They're not even saying if the
boat was his. I'm telling you it's a multiple murder.
Mafia from New York. Nothing good can come of selling every inch of lochfront to rich foreigners. They're
laundering money, and it's polluting our loch."

"Aonghas isn't American. He's as Scotch as they
come," said Ant'ny White.

"Scots," corrected Clennie scornfully for the
thousandth time. "Not Scotch, Scots. Scotch is what
Englishmen drink when they're too cheap to buy decent whisky. Scotch is a drink. Scots are a people."

"How you sometimes go o-on a-about n-nothing
Clennie," stuttered Iain Dubh, shifting in his seat
under Clennie's glare. "O-Our A-A-Aonghas is d-
drowndeded."

"Maybe they were smuggling whisky, and Aonghas
came across them, and they killed him to keep him
quiet," Clennie offered.

"Or 'shine," he continued. "They're smuggling
'shine from the old mine – I heard someone started up
Pezerello's old still. Italians. See? I'm telling you, it's
the Mafia."

*'Officials suspended search efforts as darkness fell last
evening and in the face of deteriorating conditions.
RCMP have turned things over to available search and
rescue teams, saying it was unlikely that anyone could
survive in either the water or the woods at this time of*

year. Your source for the latest news, weather and sports, 101.5 The Hawk or 1015thehawk.com. Follow us on Facebook at 1015 The Hawk.'

Wednesday mornings, many retired and underemployed middle-to-old-aged people living around this end of the loch drop in to the community hall for coffee and conversation. It's often an energized atmosphere in the hall, as small groups play cards or board games, or just swap stories, discuss the weather, test their knowledge of local genealogy, or impart tips on the latest in tractor hygiene.

Normally, the morning's howling wind and the rain-snow mix rattling the windows would be cause for discourse about leaking windows, missing shingles, climate change and the October gale of '76. But not this week.

'Despite the foul weather, searchers have redoubled their efforts this morning, following the recovery at dawn of a pair of coveralls snagged on a partially submerged log run aground at low tide near MacKenzie Point. More news at eleven at 101.5 The Hawk and www.1015thehawk. com.'

Clennie was rarely first to arrive for Wednesday morning coffee. Some say it was because he liked to make an entrance. Some think it was so no one would notice that he didn't bring any sweets as most people do during the first quarter-hour or so. Yet coming early had the benefit of sitting in a commanding seat every week. It must have been a weekly struggle to decide which purpose suited him better.

Most weeks, Clennie was incandescent with anticipation of the conversation coming around to his latest scare or scheme. But this Wednesday, he was the first one there and he was uncharacteristically subdued. He absentmindedly dropped his quarter in the dollar dish, and he didn't notice that he'd taken a seat overlooking the loch, his back to the door. This week, Clennie would not have Aonghas Fleming to argue with, and the realization that he might never again see his lifelong friend was unsettling.

One by one, the regulars blew in from the storm raging outside – everyone was soaked to the skin just coming across the parking lot. The women dutifully deposited their best efforts on the sweets table while the men dropped a few coins in the dollar dish as a voluntary entrance fee. Feet stomped off the wet, caps and coats were hung dripping on the worn hooks just inside the door resulting in growing puddles on the brittle linoleum floor.

Greetings and comments about the weather were strained as the men took their habitual seats around the table, hyperaware that Aonghas Fleming's chair was empty. Even the normally boisterous card game at the next table was muted.

Clennie sipped his tea and absentmindedly tapped the sugar dust off an oatcake.

"Any word?" he asked. It was a rhetorical question. If there was something new, he would have laid claim to it already.

Brandishing his oatcake half-heartedly, Clennie leaned forward to take up his cause. "I'm telling you," he started, "it's a drug war—"

"A-A-Aonghas!" gasped Iain Dubh.

"Yes, Aonghas," said Clennie, "but he wasn't part of it, he—"

"No! A-A-Aonghas!" Iain Dubh pointed an unsteady finger toward the rain-soaked window and the

7

parking lot as the door burst open, filling the hall with the noise and smell of the churning loch across the road filled the hall once again.

Stomping his feet, hat and hair dripping like he'd emerged from a watery grave, stood—

"A-A-Aonghas!" Iain Dubh's chair fell over with a crash as he launched toward the door. He grasped the hand and then the shoulders of their weather-worn friend, Aonghas Fleming, who, in the midst of taking off his soaking fleece jacket, froze at the sight of the choir of gaping but speechless mouths of his friends at the men's table.

"Y-you're here!"

Aonghas looked around uncertainly. "It's Wednesday. It is Wednesday, right?"

"A-Aonghas. We thought you was—"

"Late? Cheezuss, Iain Dubh – the highway's not fit this morning, and I'm after coming all the way from Halifax on the bus."

Clennie was all but motionless, trying not to choke on the oatcake half in and half out of his open mouth.

"A-Aonghas. They f-f-found your b-boat. Your coveralls. W-W-We thought—"

"What do you mean? They found my boat. Who's they?"

Clennie was trying to regain his composure, and his authority, in the midst of the attention Aonghas's resurrection had caused. "The Mounties. There was a report. Your boat. Your coveralls," he sputtered.

"What in the name of Cheezuss do the Mounties want with my boat and my coveralls? Where's my boat Clennie?"

"Drugs. Mafia. Murder." Clennie could not spit it out coherently.

"Cheezuss, Clennie – breathe. You look about to pass out."

Iain Dubh took over. "A-Aonghas. W-where've y-you been? They've been look— we've been looking for y-you for a-a week," he stuttered.

"Halifax. I was up to Halifax to visit a friend on his birthday." Looking at his best friend Clennie, he asked, "Where's my boat?"

"They found it overturned. Old Mrs. MacLean saw it keel up. And your body— a body. They found your life jacket."

"Overturned? Is it alright? Where is it? Goddammit, I put an extra line out." He got wide-eyed. "What about Angus?"

The blank faces of his friends betrayed their ignorance and their confusion.

"I just called him that. Angus. Like I said, I was going away for a few days. I didn't want anybody fishing in my spot." Still no understanding was evident.

"I anchored my boat and put a dummy in it." Still nothing.

"Like a scarecrow. So people wouldn't take my spot. I called him Angus. After my nephew." He paused.

Clennie was first to speak. "You. Dumb. F—"

"F-F-riggin' genius," interrupted Ian Dubh. "A-Aonghas Fleming, y-you're a-a-a f-f-friggin' genius."

Aonghas looked from Iain Dubh to Clennie and around the table at the others. Narrowing his eyes, he asked, "what's this about drugs?"

Clennie bristled. "Just some confusion."

"G-g-genius, p-pure g-g-genius," clucked Ian Dubh, still shaking his head in admiration as he poured his friend a coffee.

Clennie quietly pushed his chair back from the table and rose to his feet. "I gotta make a call," he said, and he strode toward the exit.

"Where's my boat, Iain Dubh?" Aonghas asked.

'The Hawk news 101.5 has learned that the RCMP have located the owner of a small boat found overturned in Loch Bras d'Or a week ago. They do not suspect foul play and consider the matter closed. If you have news to share, contact our newsroom at 101.5 The Hawk or 1015thehawk.com. That's 1015thehawk.com.'

fin

NO PLACE LIKE HOME

"Excuse me!" As she lowered the driver's-side window of her sporty SUV, a youngish and attractive woman called out to the old man standing roadside. Once the window was fully open, she added, "I'm looking for West Bay Road."

"You found it." The old fellow needlessly shortened up on the leash of the aging Sheltie at his feet. The dog flopped onto its side in exhaustion, having limped reluctantly the length of the laneway from the modest Cape Cod house behind them. The old man took an anxious puff of his single daily ration of tobacco, then politely held it behind his back.

"But the sign said this is Cenotaph Road." The woman reached over to the passenger seat and pulled a road map into position on the steering wheel, ready for directions.

"Right," he said.

"Which is it?" she asked.

"Depends."

"Depends?"

"Well now," he said, putting on his best rural brogue – the one reserved for tourists and punch-lines. "It depends if ye are lookin' for an address or the place more generally."

"I'm looking for West Bay Road."

"And you've found it."

"So I'm on West Bay Road?"

"You're *in* West Bay Road. You're *on* Cenotaph Road, though it used to be called Marble Mountain Road. And why would ye be lookin'?"

"I'm looking for someone who lives in West Bay."

"Up yon road," the old man gestured with his unshaven chin.

"Excuse me?"

Sandy Bàn MacDonald – everyone in the area knows him as Sandy Bàn – took a deep breath. "Well, I see on your wee car there," he gestured toward the roof of her car and the neon green-and-yellow kayak strapped there, "you might be looking to take yer wee boat there onto West Bay."

"At some point, yes, I hope to."

"Well then, you'll be wanting to go *on* West Bay. There's a boat launch at The Landing. 'Cept it's for locals."

"Is the boat launch on West Bay Road?"

Sandy Bàn's weather-worn face wrinkled a little in restraint, trying to not show his enjoyment at adding to her confusion.

"No, it's on Marble Mountain Road." He was conscious of the time, and of the smouldering cigarette behind his back. After fifty years without, he'd recently resumed smoking as an excuse to get out of the house and away from needless conversation. Yet, here he was in the middle of one. His home-rolled cigarette – and his break – were going up in smoke without his getting more than a puff or two.

Mind you, she was a fine–looking young woman, this wayward tourist, which straightened him up a little. Even at his advanced age, there was something about a red-haired woman.... She was likely a little north of middle-aged, so the red was more like auburn and dulled by a bit of grey, but she was a redhead in her day, he could always tell. As he was before his own carrot-coloured hair had dulled.

"Is that near Dundee?" she asked. "I plan to stay at the resort there."

"No," said Sandy Bàn. "Yes. Dundee is on West Bay – but not in West Bay."

"On West Bay Road," she pressed.

Her tormentor shook his head, 'no.'

"Dundee Road," she tried hurriedly.

"Yes. No. Dundee is on West Bay Highway. You take Cenotaph Road here from West Bay Road to West Bay. Turn right, then left."

"That's West B—"

"Highway," Sandy Bàn finished for her. The Sheltie, having stored up enough energy for the return trip and bored with the conversation, emitted something between a snort and a sigh and got slowly upright with great drama. He'd heard it all before and was ready to return to the worn carpet by the kitchen stove.

"Got it," she said, though she hadn't quite, and to change the subject, she asked, "Do you happen to know anyone by the name of Alexander MacDonald in the area?"

"Aye, some."

"Some?"

"And why would ye be lookin' for one? You from the government?"

"He might be a relative – though I've never met him."

"A relation, you say. And how would that be, then?"

"My grandmother was from … the area," she generalized, not wishing another attempt at local geography.

"Oh, aye. And where would ye be from?"

"Waltham. Near Boston. That's in Mass—"

"I knows where Boston is missy, but you don't have the accent."

"I grew up in Wisconsin. My mother was originally from Boston. She and I moved back there after my father died."

"Boston, you say." Sandy Bàn's voice trailed off as though distracted. Then – noting the dog was trying to start up the driveway – motioned to take his leave.

"You said you know someone named Alexander MacDonald?" she pressed.

"Oh, aye, I knows some," Sandy Bàn replied matter-of-factly to conceal his curiosity.

"Some?" she echoed, before she could catch herself.

"There's no small number of MacDonalds between here and The Points of West Bay," he said, "and Alexander being a proper Scots name, there's no small number of them. What's his father's name?"

"Actually, I don't know for sure. My mother told me she has, or had, cousins in these parts. Her mother – my grandmother – used to tell her stories about Cape Breton. Though my mother never visited, she insisted I come someday. I had to promise her."

"What was your grandmother's name then."

"She was a MacDonald. She married a Campbell."

"Not surprised they had to move to Boston. The MacDonalds and the Campbells," he paused, adopting a sympathetic look, "don't get along too well. You know how it is."

"Like the Hatfields and McCoys."

"Eh? No. No Hatfields 'round here, but there was a McCoy down in Orangedale some time ago."

"No, I mean— it was a famous family feud. In the States. Not sure where it comes from or if it's even a true story. From a book, maybe."

"Like the Macdonalds and Campbells," offered Sandy Bàn. "Well, like I say, there's plenty of MacDonalds. You're bound to find the right one if you have enough time."

"I'm off, then. Thank you." She raised a hand from the steering wheel, half in salute, half in defeat, before powering the window up against the evening air and the black flies that had by now found her.

Sandy Bàn turned to return up the driveway and back inside, where his sister was no doubt warming up to resume their conversation. "*Chac,*" he muttered, throwing his now-unsalvageable smoke to the gravel in disgust.

He turned to watch as the Boston car drove off in the wrong direction. Sure enough, before he'd rounded the corner of the house to the back door, the Boston redhead drove by again and with a little toot of the horn headed in the right direction.

"Tourists," he chuckled to no one in particular.

"Woof," rasped the Sheltie as if to agree.

∞∞

Checking in at the front desk of Dundee Resort, Sabella Sandusky – Sibby, to her family and friends – asked the young clerk if she was local.

"Not for much longer, I hope," the clerk responded. without lifting her eyes from her screen.

Sibby looked up from her registration card and studied the girl, who was squinting at the computer screen in front of her. "Lexie," according to her name tag, had thick red hair and a constellation of matching freckles. She was a little on the heavy side, but not overly so. Maybe a few freshman pounds from university.

It crossed Sibby's mind that Lexie could have been her at a younger age, however worn the notion of a lost and distant incarnation of herself might be. 'The stuff of too many novels,' she thought, and shook it off.

"My family came from these parts, apparently," Sibby offered as small talk. "Can you recommend anyone I might speak with about local history?"

"Not really." Lexie still didn't look up from her task.

"My mother told me I might have a cousin around here somewhere. I thought maybe I'd try to find him."

"Is he old too?" Lexie blushed and scrambled to recover. "I mostly know only people my age and my family, though every time I meet someone, I'm told we are related somehow. I don't pay too much attention. If you have one relative here, you may have a hundred, and you can't do anything without your grandmother knows."

"Tell me," Sibby changed the subject as she took her room key and picked up her bag. "I have a kayak with me. Can you recommend some place I can launch it and maybe explore a bit?"

"There's a beach across the road there," Lexie tipped her head in the direction of the loch, "but if the wind is blowing, which is almost always, it can be tough to get anywhere. People around here mostly use the boat launch at The Landing of West Bay. It's more sheltered. If anyone asks, just say you have relatives here – that makes it okay. But me and my friends go to the beach at Marble Mountain."

∞∞

The boat launch at The Landing is within sight of the Post Office and across the road from a storefront signed "Harmony Gifts, Crafts, Café," the name centred between two folksy paintings of smiling pigs. A narrow front porch running the width of the store facing the cove displayed an assortment of folk art: knotted and twisted driftwood cleverly pieced together to form a whimsical bicycle stood next to something that more or less depicted a giraffe, or perhaps an octopus, or maybe a llama – also of driftwood. Two woven willow garden chairs sat lopsidedly on either side of a gaily painted lobster trap. On top of that was fixed a slab of wood completing a low table. On either side of the entrance to the store stood life-size pot-bellied pigs – surprisingly lifelike, given the other primitive objects – matching those on the sign overhead, their faces framed by crinoline collars, like ballerina tutus, one pink, one blue.

It was early, and nothing seemed to be open yet, so Sibby unloaded her kayak and placed it on a grassy area above the gravel slip next to a decrepit jetty. A small sign warned "Private Launch," but taking Lexie's advice to heart, Sibby readied her gear anyway – paddle, flotation vest, snacks, camera – and it didn't take her long to set out on the morning calm of the cove.

Sibby hadn't kayaked a lot – can kayak be a verb, she wondered to herself? She'd purchased the brightly coloured craft on a whim a few years back, planning, at the time, to make a few changes in her life, including more fresh air and exercise.

She'd not made a plan for this morning – for the entire trip, for that matter – but felt the need for a few minutes of natural solitude. She'd enjoyed travelling solo alright, but the hum of tires on pavement, the constant search for radio signals and eating alone in diners and bars beneath a cacophony of baseball, pre-season hockey and bobble-headed sports commentators was hardly soothing. In Dundee last evening the hubbub of some sort of men's golf mixer next to the hotel had made for a restless night; it was hardly the homecoming she'd romanticized as the miles whined beneath her tires.

A few dozen strokes into the cove, Sibby rested her paddle across her lap and glided silently, watching as life along the edges looked back at her with suspicion – ready to fly, swim or scurry away – but resuming their furtive foraging at her passing. A kingfisher rocketed from an overhanging branch, returning from the surface of the water in a flash of silver and blue. A pair of herons waded haughtily in the shallows still steaming from contact with early morning sunbeams. This is what she thought the kayak would buy her. Balance. Stillness. Silence. Thunder?

A deep, protracted rumble in the unseen distance broke her reverie, and she swung the kayak back around toward her car in anticipation of rain. The rumble came again. Closer, more menacing, despite the blue sky all around. Gently slipping from the scene as unobtrusively as she had entered, Sibby eyed the ridge of mountains running northward parallel with the shore of the loch. At any moment a bank of dark clouds would roll over the top and cascade down the sides.

The rumble kept coming. Louder and without pause when, suddenly, a humungous camouflaged pickup truck roared into view. Its obviously custom – and likely illegal – exhaust system beat out a crescendo of kettle drums as it came down the hill into the village. Herons, geese and ducks clamoured skyward in protest as the truck thundered past Harmony Gifts. The driver's double-clutch shift to take the incline at the other end of the village rattled the brittle windows of the rundown tavern next door. The rumbling continued as the truck took the hill away from the village toward town.

In her relatively affluent suburb of Boston, Sibby had learned to live with the boom! boom! boom! of expensive sub-woofers in souped-up Honda Civics rattling her windows as they passed. But this! And why anyone would camouflage a truck that was as loud as a battlefield was beyond the pale. It was a scene right out of *The Dukes of Hazard*.

Having by now paddled most of the way back to her car at the boat launch anyway, Sibby decided to call it quits for now. The post office would surely open soon. There she could continue her inquiries about Alexander MacDonald, after a visit to the gift shop. She unconsciously glanced to the shop in confirmation. There was something different there, though she couldn't quite put her finger on it.

Gliding nearer, she was startled by the sudden appearance of a man from the tall bushes at the water's edge, just to the left of the boat slip. He'd obviously been fishing, but if he was there when she launched, Sibby had failed to notice. Pleasantly but silently, the man gently laid his hands on the prow of the kayak and guided it to the slip.

"Good morning. Thank You." Sibby hitched herself up, slung her right foot out of the cockpit and into the water. She stood up, her left leg following rather more gracefully than usual, thanks to the steadying hand of the stranger. Paddle in one hand and the kayak's nylon tether in the other, she pulled the boat farther up the gravel and onto the grass next to it. She waved off the mute offer of further assistance, proceeded to organize her things and prepare the roof rack to receive the kayak. When she turned around, the fisherman had blended once more into the bushes and weeds below the road.

As she fussed with the straps to secure the kayak Sibby sensed movement across the road, and from the corner of her eye, saw that the gift shop was being readied for the day. Looking up fully a few moments later, she saw that a tall thin woman with long straight salt-and-pepper hair was now standing in the doorway looking over the cove as if taking inventory of the unfolding morning. At her feet sat one of the colourful pigs that earlier had bookended the shop's front porch.

"Good morning," the woman hollered. "Some day!"

Sibby opened her mouth to respond in kind but shut up mid breath when the pig suddenly came to life. It stood up, waddled to the edge of the porch and looked right at her. Its pink ruffed collar stood straight up, just like in the portraits on the sign overhead.

"Don't mind Sander, there." The woman nodded toward the unseen fisherman in the weeds. "He's a man of few words. That's rare around here, so be thankful."

Sibby jerked her head up with a smile to signify that she got the joke, and stepped back to survey her readiness. Everything in order, she locked the car and headed across the road toward the shop – her demeanour a mixture of curiosity, purpose and wariness of the pig. The porch was deserted now, but the door was wide open, and she could hear the pitter-patter of little pig feet from within.

Stepping up onto the porch, Sibby removed her sunglasses for a better look at the folkart. The shop-keeper had also set out a number of colourful whirli-gigs and wind chimes. The latter consisted of pieces of driftwood and other found objects: bits of ribbon, old tarnished spoons and pieces of corroded copper pipe. These rattled and clunked rather unharmoniously in the morning breeze.

The moment she crossed the doorway into the store, a rasping voice called out, "Ding dong. Hallo."

Standing firmly on all fours, the pig was looking her up and down, nostrils and crinoline twitching as it sniffed in greeting. Her passage thus hindered, Sibby looked around the sparsely furnished interior, half looking for a reason to go on, half looking for a reason to turn and leave. The shop was a great deal larger than it appeared from the road.

"Hallo. *Maduinn mhath. Bonjour,*" chimed the squeaky voice. Sibby eyed the pig skeptically – knowing yet wondering.

"Good morning," called a female voice. The shopkeeper approached from the rear of the store, wiping her hands on a purple apron on which was screened the same pig portrait as on the sign outside.

"I see you met Harmony. Don't worry; she's clean and friendly." She dropped to her haunches to scratch the pig under its chin.

"Hallo. *Ciamar a tha thu. Pjlas'i.*" Sibby looked down at the pig, Harmony, and at her host.

"Thank you Hamish," the woman called over her shoulder without looking up. "*Tapadh leat.*"

Looking beyond the crouching owner, Sibby was relieved to see that Harmony was not, in fact, a talking pig. On a substantial shoulder-high bark-less tree trunk with one short, thick branch jutting out, was perched a very large parrot. On its head was a tiny tam o' shanter. "Hallo," the parrot said, cocking its head as if to get a better look. "Tea's on. *Srùbag.* Tea and cake. Tea and cake."

"Coffee too, if you'd prefer," the shop owner said as she got to her feet. "Would you like some? Fresh biscuits." She twitched her head by way of pointing to a corner of the store and a small assortment of mismatched tables and chairs, a couple of which were well-worn upholstered armchairs. Tacked to a rough wooden beam overhead, hand-painted signs identified not only "The Café" but "The Library," "The Museum" and the "WC." Each sign bore the small pig graphics.

"The Museum" likely lived a former life as a jeweller's display case, but instead of artifacts, it displayed an enormous assortment of pig figurines and pig-themed knickknacks. From the corner of her eye, Sibby could see, or perhaps sense, the store's pig watching her. She imagined the pig beaming proudly at this stranger's interest in the display, though Sibby resisted the urge to turn and confirm.

"The Library" was a collection of second and third, perhaps even fourth-hand books of every description and condition arranged neatly but randomly in a glass-less display case. A cursory reconnaissance revealed someone's selective interests: *Holistic Tarot, Spiritual Balance, The Pocket Companion to Healing Crystals, Pigs as Pets, Dracula's Balls.*

Still uncertain whether to sit or to be on her way, Sibby heard the pitter-patter of pig feet heading quickly for the front door again, just as the shop's feathered door chime loosed another raspy "Hallo. *Maduinn mhath.*"

"*Maduinn mhath*, Hamish." A man's voice drawled, "*Comhaire a thu?*"

"*Gla mha. Gla mha,*" the parrot squawked.

Backlit by the door and windows, their appearances lacking detail, the silhouettes of two elderly gentlemen approached the rear of the store where Sibby was examining an assortment of sea glass, sea shells and sea-smoothed pebbles on which were painted simplistic flowers, frogs, feathers and pigs. The hand-painted pigs emulated those on the sign outside – one pink (obviously Harmony) and one blue. Beneath each was printed their name. The blue pig was, apparently, called Toto. Sibby wondered if Toto would show itself at some point.

Overhead, a collection of dreamcatchers fussed in the wake of the two men as they passed behind her into the café area. Harmony tap-tapped past them and around a corner to some unseen activity.

Behind her, Sibby heard two chairs scraped across the worn wooden floor. She turned as the men noisily hitched themselves closer to a small square table fashioned from reclaimed wood and driftwood.

"Coffee's on," the singsong voice of the proprietor called from somewhere nearby. "Help yourselfs. I'll be there directly."

"I'll keep an eye on John-Duncan here, Pretty," called the taller of the men. "Make sure he don't steal nothin'." The speaker sat with his back to Sibby – the other man faced her. A handsome man in his day, she thought. His bright blue eyes twinkled beneath bushy brows still remarkably black given his nearly white mane of hair. His neck and ears bristled with coarse wisps of grey.

The shopkeeper's voice gave a sharp laugh. "He's not the one I worry about Sandy Bàn. Help yourselfs – fresh biscuits on the way."

Pretty, as Sibby now knew her, emerged carrying a well-used aluminum tray piled high with biscuits. She crossed the little room and set the tray on a glass counter next to the coffee and tea pots. Above the arrangement was a large map which Sibby recognized was of the local area.

"Leave some for the tourist, will you fellas?" she teased.

Turning her attention to Sibby once more, she wiped her hands on the purple pig apron. "Now," she said, "what can we do for you? What brings you to The Landing?"

Sibby put down the stained glass fairy she'd been examining and looked at her host. "Just visiting. I'm from the U.S. Some of my family came from around here apparently – a long time ago."

"We get a lot of visitors like that. Don't we fellas?" Pretty was focused on Sibby, but had picked up the carafe of coffee and was taking it over to the two men, the taller of whom had now turned more in her direction. She recognized him from yesterday's conversation on West Bay Road – no, *in* West Bay Road.

"Hello again," she greeted the man she now knew as Sandy.

He looked at her blankly for a second before recognition set in. Their reunion didn't merit a smile, apparently, but he wasn't unfriendly either.

"Boston," he jerked his head slightly to acknowledge Sibby for the other man – John-Duncan – and informed him of the previous evening's encounter.

Sandy Bàn turned back to Sibby. "Grandmother's cousin was it? John-Duncan here knows most of the families in these parts. Maybe he knows your grandmother's cousin."

John-Duncan's eyes scanned Sibby in a familiar Highland appraisal that fell somewhere between superiority, contempt and amusement.

"Her grandmother was from here. MacDonald. Married a Campbell," Sandy Bàn told his friend, adding a nod. "Moved to the Boston States." Sandy Bàn had a knowing look in his eyes at the mention of the union, which was met by a nod of understanding followed by a sympathetic little shake of the head.

"Well, miss..."

"Sibby," she filled in.

"Sibby," John-Duncan repeated.

"Short for Sabella," she said helpfully.

"A good Hebridean name," nodded Sandy Bàn. John-Duncan hesitated, half-expecting his friend to continue. He didn't, so Sibby did.

"My mother thought there might still be family around here," she offered. She remained standing, one hand unconsciously tracing the pattern on a pressed-back chair.

"Mind these two," Pretty said as she breezed by. "They don't know the difference between history, her story and just plain stories."

"That's no way to talk about your best customers, Pretty," John-Duncan said, feigning hurt.

"That'd be true of paying customers, John-Duncan," she shot back, emphasizing the *paying*, with a wink to include Sibby in the exchange. "That fella knows lots of local history; he's your best bet if he gets around to it."

"Who is it you're looking for, Sweety?" John-Duncan took a sip from his mug.

"Sibby," she asserted. "Alexander MacDonald."

"Dead or alive?" asked John-Duncan matter-of-factly.

"Excuse me?"

"Well, you say this MacDonald fellow is – or was – your grandmother's cousin. That'd make him pretty old, considering. No offence. So, dead most likely. There's more dead than alive around here anyways.

"Now, if your Alexander MacDonald is still alive, you might have a chance. If he's dead, maybe half a chance. It's tradition to name a boy after his paternal grandfather, so finding the right Alexander MacDonald about your age might lead you to your grandmother's cousin's grandson – your cousin too. Then you trace backwards to learn about the grandfather."

Concentrating on what she was being told, Sibby hadn't noticed Harmony joining the conversation, and she jumped when the pig brushed up against her legs.

"Just looking for attention, she is." Pretty looked over from across the store. "Give her a little scratch under her chinny-chin-chin, and you'll be her friend for life. But don't give her any treats, she's on a special diet."

"So, it's true there may be more than one?" Sibby asked John-Duncan as she attended to Harmony's need for attention.

"More than true Sally. It's a fact."

"Sibby."

"Right."

Sandy Bàn drained his mug in a way that signalled he was about to adjourn. John-Duncan motioned as though he might follow suit but settled again, looking studious.

"'Course," he started, "if your grandmother's cousin is dead, and if he didn't have a son who had a son, there mightn't be a young cousin Alexander. And if your grandmother's cousin had a daughter, and she married and had a son, he might still be named Alexander, but maybe not MacDonald. D'ye ken?"

Sibby squinted in concentration, which brought another nudge from Harmony, who gave a quiet snort of satisfaction when Sibby resumed her absentminded scratching.

"Ding dong! Hallo! *Madiunn mha* Joanie!" the door parrot squawked, alerting everyone that another customer had stepped through the doorway.

"Morning Joanie," Pretty called across the shop in acknowledgement. "There's more coffee on in the back if those two drained the last one."

A middle-aged woman in a postal-worker uniform strode into view carrying a large travel mug.

"Morning John-Duncan. Morning Sandy Bàn. Still can't boil water on your own, I see."

Sandy Bàn made a great show of looking at his wristwatch. "Had lots of time to kill waiting for the post office to open."

Joanie loosed a generous laugh, set her own mug down on the counter, and poured the last of the coffee with a confident cascade.

"Morning," she acknowledged Sibby. "And *maduinn mha* to you miss piggy." The pig gave a little snort that sounded to Sibby like indignation.

It must have struck Joanie like that too, for she gave a loud laugh and bent down to chuck Harmony under the chin. "Don't get your snout out of joint, piggy. You knows I loves ya."

Pretty reappeared with a full carafe. "Lovely day, Joanie. Not a cloud in the sky, not a care in the world."

"We'll take it," chimed the postmaster. "One more, one less, *seanmhair* used to say. My grandmother," she added for Sibby's benefit.

"This lady is wanting to find a long-lost relative," Pretty nodded toward Sibby. "I was hoping these two could help, but—"

"But nothin'," John-Duncan growled. Then, cracking a smile, he added graciously, "we're just getting to know the lass so we can situate her proper."

"I planned to go to your post office too," Sibby confirmed. "I thought you might have a good handle on people in the area."

"Not too bad. I know who is living where around the bay, of course, and I've lived here most of my life, so I might be able to help. I have to be careful though – privacy and all."

"Of course."

"Don't let that fool you," John-Duncan said. "There's more news than mail goes through that little post office."

"Come over after you're done here dear. We'll see what we can do." With that, the postmaster turned and headed for the door, almost tripping over Harmony as she did.

"Oops, sorry piggy. See you fellas. Don't forget to mail a few cards and letters the old-fashioned way. My pension's not paid up yet."

Sandy Bàn and John-Duncan seemed about to leave too, so Sibby thought she would shop a little more to allow a few minutes before she followed along to the post office. Before the men made it to the door, however, John-Duncan turned and came back to her. Sandy Bàn kept going across to the Post Office, presumably.

Adjusting his trousers in that way that older men do, John-Duncan struck a thoughtful pose and, after hesitating a moment as though summoning his faculties, told her he'd give it all some thought.

"See, the problem is we're missing a generation of information. It's true there are plenty of MacDonalds and not a few Alexanders among them, but that may not be enough. What'd you say was your grandmother's name? I can't remember if you told me."

"Sabella Campbell. That was her married name. She was a MacDonald."

"What's her father's name?"

"Truth be told, I don't know for certain, but I believe it was Alisdair. I gather he disowned her when she married. Apparently, she spoke fondly of her childhood and of the village, but refused to speak about her parents – not even to my mother. She – my grandmother – never returned to Cape Breton, my mother never visited either."

"Not much to go on girlie."

"I have an old picture." Sibby slipped her purse strap from her shoulder with her left hand and held it high so she could reach into the bag with her right. She was suddenly cognizant of the designer bag's incongruity with her surroundings. If it registered with John-Duncan, he didn't let on.

A faded cardboard folder retrieved from her bag revealed an equally faded and somewhat torn tissue paper, which in turn protected a yellowed photograph in a once-gilded frame. You could see where the photo was stuck to the glass in places it had gotten wet. In the photo, two young men posed beside a horse-and-buggy in front of a large wood-shingled building. Its faded and peeling sign advertised MacPhie Carriage Makers. Scrawled with a heavy hand, near the bottom of the photograph, you could make out most of an inscription: 'no place l ke om' – 'No Place Like Home' maybe?

Sibby held out the photograph to John-Duncan.

"This is all I have to go on. I know it seems strange but it's all I have of her, and all she had of Cape Breton, of this place. Whatever came between her and her family must have been deep and wide. So far as I know, this is the only thing she kept from her early life."

"You show this to old Sandy Bàn when you met him?" John-Duncan asked.

"Um, no. Our conversation last evening was rather brief – this morning's too."

"He's a man of few words until he warms to you. If he warms to you. Show him the picture. He's just gone for his mail."

"His name is Sandy, right? Short for Alexander? I don't sup...."

"No lassie. The MacDonalds—"

"Sandy MacDonald!" Sibby interrupted. "Why didn't he say so? Short for Alexander? Alexander MacDonald?"

"No. Yes. He's a MacDonald, right enough, William Alexander, truth. But that's not where he gets the 'Sandy' from. That comes from his mother, Alexandra MacDonald. Beautiful woman, Sandy. Young William was her spittin' image, 'cept more manly as he got older."

"Does that happen often? Names I mean."

"No. Yes, girlie, all the time. Here, he was over in West Bay Road when you met? Visiting his sister Alexa, no doubt. She was married to Collie Sandy MacDonald."

"For Colin Alexander?" Sibby asked, thinking she was catching on. It seemed logical enough.

"Yes. No. Sort of. See, his name was Alexander MacDonald. He's dead now like I said – did I? His mother's name was Colleen. She was a MacKenzie from Lime Hill. Her family called her Collie. Her son, Alexander, the one who was married to Sandy Bàn's sister, was Collie Sandy, see?"

She didn't see – not clearly, anyway – but she gave John-Duncan a polite nod that she hoped would end the lesson for now.

"But you think Mr. MacDonald – Sandy Bàn – might recognize the people in the picture?"

"I could be wrong, so it's better he looks at it. I daresay he will if he takes his time. You catch up to him if you can. Otherwise, come here at the same time tomorrow, and we'll see what he says."

He called out a farewell to unseen Pretty. "Bye girlie. Say hello to your father for us."

∞∞

The next morning was too windy for kayaking. Sibby recognized that her lack of experience and her lack of upper body strength would make venturing out on the water rather risky. Too early for the gift shop, she continued the drive through The Landing and onward toward Marble Mountain.

It was a stunning drive that autumn morning. The sun reflecting off the loch turned its numerous small islands into silhouettes. A bald eagle rode an updraft almost parallel with the road, matching the car's sight-seeing speed, unhurried and as yet unharried by crows, all scouting shoreline homes for scraps and small pets.

Sibby too was unhurried, pulled along by some invisible force answering to an inner directive. When she finally pulled over and got out of her car at the lookout – lookoff, the sign said – just beyond Marble Mountain village, the eagle passed right in front of her as it continued its silent, effortless cruise. Sibby was sure it turned its head and studied her deeply, and she was momentarily overcome, drawing a sharp breath as though roused from a momentary trance.

The view from the Marble Mountain lookoff is memorable. From that vantage point on a clear day, the white sandy beach borders crystal clear azure waters that belie the post-industrial slag heaps that overshadow them. The revealing slip-of-the-tongue by the front desk clerk at the resort, Lexie, came to her unexpectedly. Lexie and her friends came here sometimes, she had said, and Sibby wondered if they appreciated the rare gifts of such a place. 'Not for much longer,' Lexie had said. Sibby shook her head – at once understanding and lamenting the restlessness of youth.

∞∞

Back in The Landing, the village was coming alive when Sibby pulled onto the grassy verge across from Harmony Gifts. On reaching the top step of the veranda, she was welcomed once more by the pig, which today was sporting glittering nail polish. She lifted a front hoof in greeting, but Sibby imagined it was to show off her manicure.

"*Maduinn mhath*," squawked Hamish.

"Good morning," Sibby replied as she entered the store and walked past the parrot toward the café at the rear.

"Here's the lass we was talking about. Look here, Susie, we brought reinforcements. This here's Ollie – Olaf Balderston. But we call him Bothersome."

Balderston gave her a nod and a toothy smile in acknowledgement. The man's chiselled features would make Kirk Douglas blush, she thought. Though he was much younger than the other two men – his bristle of platinum-blonde almost white hair and weathered face might fool a quick glance – he seemed at home in their midst. Sibby judged he was closer to her age.

"Ollie here has taken quite an interest in local history since moving here, what three, four years ago? I keep telling him he should write a book. Sharp as a tack, he is."

Sandy Bàn snickered. "So sharp, some call him Olfa, like the knife."

John-Duncan jumped in. "Sometimes he's full of shit and we call him Offal." Balderston scratched his chin with his middle finger in silent rebuttal.

"Nice to meet you Suze," he smiled. He turned his attention to the smartphone cradled in both his hands and scrolled the screen purposefully with his right thumb. "Here it is. I told you. It says here that human flatulence – that's farts to you old farts – contributes to global warming." His icy blue eyes sparkled in amusement at sharing the news, and he gave John-Duncan an exaggerated pat on the shoulder as if to encourage him. "So put a cork in 'er b'ye! I got to outlive ya's."

John-Duncan held out his left hand to take the phone and read the evidence for himself. He reached out blindly with his right hand to Sandy Bàn, saying, "give us your glasses a minute will you? I can't read these little words."

Sandy Bàn took a pair of eyeglasses out of his shirt pocket and handed them over. "Just try to remember where you got 'em," he said.

John-Duncan responded, "my memory's just fine – it's you we're all worried about. Cheezuss! Clean these once in a while will you? They're a disgrace!"

"Serves you right for not cleaning my teeth the last time you used them," Sandy Bàn said, watching to gauge Sibby's reaction, "you know I hate ketchup."

Ollie winked at her. "Like an old married couple, aren't they?"

As John-Duncan looked over the evidence with Ollie's help, Sandy Bàn pulled on the seat of the vacant chair next to him and motioned for Sibby to sit.

"Now, Sibby." He patted the seat of the chair, saying, "this old fart here tells me you have a special picture he thinks I should take a look at."

Sibby was surprised that he called her by name. Their previous encounters being relatively brief, she thought he was disinterested, even a little aloof.

As she sat, she reached into her purse and retrieved the photo, still folded into the yellowed tissue paper, which she unwrapped before handing it over. As Sandy Bàn took it from her, John-Duncan held out the eyeglasses to him. "You'll be needing these back *bodach*. Wouldn't want you to make a mistake."

Sandy Bàn put the glasses on the tip of his nose and took the frame from Sibby, turning it right side up as he shifted on his seat for better light.

"This wasn't yesterday," he said with a shake of his head. "The Landing was a busy place in those days – not that I'm old enough to remember. John-Duncan here might." Sibby had thought John-Duncan was actually the younger of the pair. Sandy Bàn continued.

"You say this is your Alexander MacDonald? Was?"

"I didn't say that," Sibby replied, "I just thought it might be, since it was among my grandmother's things."

"Well, this fellow on the right bears a strong resemblance to John-Alec Campbell in Lime Hill. But the carriage maker closed in the 1920s; my eldest brother, Sandy Neal, ran his livery business out of there for years, so it's not him – not John-Alec Campbell, I mean."

"Sandy Neal?" she asked, looking to Ollie for confirmation.

He shook his head. His grin said, 'don't ask.'

"John-Alex Campbell?" Sibby repeated. "Another Alexander?"

"Yes. No. Alec, not Alex," said Sandy Bàn. "What'd you think John-Duncan? Much younger. If it wasn't for the building and carriage, you'd swear it's he."

"I thought so too, but I didn't want to say," John-Duncan replied.

Sibby looked at them in turn. "Lime Hill. That's on the way to Marble Mountain?"

"That's right girlie," answered Sandy Bàn. Then, looking at John-Duncan, "who's the other fellow, I wonder? Don't resemble anyone I know." The second figure's features were partially obscured by shadows, making positive identification more difficult.

As Sibby took back the photograph, Sandy Bàn shook his head and gave a little 'tsk tsk.' "A MacDonald and a Campbell – no surprise they never came back."

He looked at John-Duncan, and with a twinkle in his eye, told him, "I don't know how you can sleep."

Ollie laughed. "Cheezuss. Glen Coe was over 400 years ago – get over it man!"

John-Duncan, feigning hurt, countered that it was Sandy Bàn who shouldn't sleep too soundly. "You never know who your friends are, b'y. Better watch your back."

Though unfamiliar with whatever historical griev-ance was being referenced, it was obvious to Sibby that it was all in jest. Still, she was relieved when Ollie inter-jected, holding out his smartphone so Sibby could see that he'd opened Google maps for her reference. "This is John-Alec's place."

"Thanks," she said. After looking she handed Ollie's phone back to him.

∞∞

The signage along the unnumbered road between The Landing and Marble Mountain identifies settlements so dwindled in population that placenames hardly seem necessary. But there's more here than meets the eye, visible to none but older locals. Overgrown roads lined with feral apple trees being slowly starved out by alders, and crowded out by fast-growing spruce trees, dissect the steep hillside overlooking the loch.

Sibby proceeded cautiously, dodging the potholes and patches she'd earlier fallen victim to, as she watched for a mailbox with the name Campbell. "You can't miss it," Ollie had told her. "It's about ten minutes from here."

Sibby wondered under what conditions the duration of the journey was recorded – dirt, gravel, paved or their present state – for it was nearly twenty-five minutes before she found the mailbox she was looking for.

∞∞

John-Alec Campbell did indeed resemble the man in the picture, who, as it turned out, was his own father, John-Alec. And the youngish man next to him outside MacPhie's?

"Might be my uncle. John-John – I don't know much about him," he said, "He disappeared. First picture I ever saw of him, if it's he. I was named for him."

"But wasn't your father's name John-Alec?"

"That's right dear. John-Alec was my father – Iain Alec Campbell on his death certificate – and John-John was my uncle. Brother Jack they called him, since he was always destined to be a man of the cloth. Went off to train for the ministry, but nobody heard much from him after he hooked up with the MacDonald lass.

"You're named for him? But you're called John-Alec?"

"That's how I'm known. It's less confusing."

Sibby thought otherwise, opposite, in fact, but she refrained from interrupting again.

"Between you and me, Missy, there was whispers about him runnin' off with a Catholic – a nun. The two of them were caught defrocked, so to speak, and got their wings clipped. A match made in heaven, eh?" He slapped his thigh at his play on words. "I got into more than one scrape in the schoolyard defending his name whenever some wisenheimer made a crack about it.

"But, I can't be sure," he added hurriedly. "You know how people talk – even when they don't talk. Nobody in the family ever said nothin'. Boston, you say."

Sibby thought about this for a moment. She knew even less than John-Alec Campbell did, yet couldn't help but think that family silence confirmed some sort of disgrace that would explain a rift. John-John Campbell – Brother Jack – was quite possibly her grandfather Jack. It would make sense. If so, this man, John-Alec Campbell, was her ... cousin.

"Nobody left to help you, girlie. They're all gone 'cept me – and you, if you're related, I guess. I got a few pictures you can see, if you like."

She thought about it but declined for now. "I'd like that another day, Mr. Campbell."

"John-Alec," he reminded her. "You know where to find me."

∞∞

Sibby and Ollie had earlier agreed to meet for a drink and supper in the pub at the resort.

"Where do you come from Ollie?"

"How far back would you like to go? I grew up in Newcastle. Studied in Edinburgh. My father was from a village not too far from Edinburgh – my mother was Orkadian."

"French?"

"Not Acadian, Orkadian – from Orkney. Her family was of Norwegian descent."

"Olaf."

"Right. But I'm no saint. Fish-and-chips is good."

"Good to know. From your accent, I would have guessed you are from around here."

"Growing up in the north of England, Scots father, Orkadian mother, living in Cape Breton – I kind of absorb accents around me. You don't have a Boston accent either."

"No, I grew up in Wisconsin, but moved to Boston with my mother some years ago. That's where she was from."

"And her parents were from here? John-Duncan said they – your parents – fell out with their families and never came back?"

"My grandparents, actually. That's what I was told. You said you studied here, but that must have been some time ago."

"Gee thanks." Ollie feigned hurt, but continued.

"Yeh, while doing Celtic Studies at Edinburgh. One of my professors was doing research on Gaelic folk songs and stories here in Cape Breton, and it made the place sound so charming I arranged to do my thesis here – on the Scots diaspora. It turned into two years."

"They said you'd been here four years or so."

"To make a long story short, some years later I found myself ... in need of a change and came back here – about five years ago. Got a job teaching at the community college."

"You have family with you?"

"No. All alone."

Sibby wasn't sure if there was a subtext to the "all" in his statement but chose to leave that for now.

She was surprised to find that she was quite comfortable with the Norse-Scotsman, despite their having met just that morning. She sensed that they had in common that were both outsiders.

"I must say that it feels strange to be here," Sibby confided, "in Cape Breton, I mean. On one hand I have absolutely no sense of connection with these people. At the same time, somehow the place speaks to me, as though my ancestors are calling to me from beyond the grave. Like that inscription on the photograph: 'there's no place like home.' You must think that's silly."

"Not at all, Dorothy," Ollie laughed. Then, leaning a little forward in interest, continued. "It can do that to you. I have no blood ties with this place either, yet I have the feeling that somehow I am indeed connected, or will be. Weird. I guess I'll have to stick around until I find out why. Speaking of which, how long will you be staying, do you think?"

Sibby had no idea and no set schedule, and she said so. "To be honest, I'm kind of at loose ends these days. I was looking after my mother for the last few years, and now she's gone. I don't have family responsibilities. I guess I'm looking for ... I don't know what. I have the house in Boston, but I'm divorced, and my daughter has her own life out west. My work is quite portable, so I'm not tied to any particular place or job – or even country – if I find a reason to make a change.

"I don't know what brought me here other than a promise I made to my mother," she continued. "If I ever have grandchildren, it would be good to know more about their extended family and roots than I did growing up. I confess that I had a notion that I might belong here. Silly, right?"

"Maybe you do belong here." Ollie blushed slightly, surprised by his sentimentality. "God knows The Landing needs new blood."

"I'm both a MacDonald and a Campbell," Sibby said with a laugh. "I could definitely fit in somewhere."

"Bad mixture there," Ollie laughed. "How can you live with yourself?"

"John-Alec Campbell grew up with the story that my grandparents were both destined for lives in the Church. Her a nun. But they fell in love and ran off to the States."

"Quite the love story."

"You'd think it would be cause for celebration rather than a feud."

"That's Highlanders for you – most people hereabouts are descended from Highland Scots – a proud and stubborn lot. The majority here were Presbyterian. But there were Catholics, some MacDonalds among them. Not much mixing of the two except the odd scrape outside the dances and such."

"John-Duncan was trying to explain names and nicknames, though I'm not sure I got it all. Is everyone here named Alexander, or John, or some derivative?"

"That's why everyone has a nickname. To keep everyone sorted."

"Pretty – and you – the only exceptions?"

"You'd think so, but you'd be wrong. Alexis Priscilla MacDonald – Pretty comes from a juvenile pronunciation."

"You're not serious."

"I am serious."

"So, Sandy, Sandy Bàn, Neil Sandy, Collie Sandy, Sander, Pretty, Lexie, Alex, Alisdair. All Alexander derivatives. What is this place, Stepford?"

"And, let's see, John, Joanie, Sean, Shamus, all from Iain. You get used to it."

"Does anyone know why?"

"Not really sure of all the traditions of naming your children – all of them, it seems sometimes – the same. It's not like they're related, though many are, and it's not like their birth certificate is going to match the names they use. They are likely honouring an ancestor."

Their fish-and-chips arrived. They ordered another beer each, and between bites continued their conversation. It was up to Sibby to break the silence.

"I hesitate to ask. Do nicknames sometimes apply to villages too? Like The Landing and West Bay Road?"

"Ha! That one's a puzzle, isn't it? West Bay is a body of water – the west bay of Loch Bras d'Or. West Bay is also a village, though everyone here knows it as The Landing on West Bay, The Landing for short. Now, West Bay Highway is the road from St. Peter's to West Bay, but everyone knows it as Dundee Road, which makes a lot more sense.

"Then, there's West Bay Road," he continued, "a place, not a road at all. Years ago there was a busy railway stop there, where people and freight would get off for the Post Road to The Landing – West Bay – and onward to Marble Mountain. The stop was called West Bay Road, and so is the village that grew up around it. Oh, and Marble Mountain is not where the marble mine was – that's in River Denys."

"Why don't they get that sorted?" Sibby shook her head. "It's confusing."

"Only to outsiders, so no one cares. Besides, there's nothing the Scots like better than a bit of knowledge to lord over you.

"See," he continued, "Cape Breton is like an inside joke. Though it's no joke, and they're full of them. You have to live here to get it – the joke, I mean.

"Just don't be too quick to share your joke or a laugh. They love to laugh at themselves but don't want others to get it. And they certainly don't tolerate others telling of the jokes."

"And have a bit of fun with visitors," Sibby added.

"No doubt. But they're lovable in their own right."

Sibby sensed that Ollie was getting restless, or maybe she was projecting her own fatigue, so she fidgeted with her napkin a bit and drank down the last of her beer. Ollie obliged by sitting back in his seat a little. Their conversation was nearing an end for the day.

Pausing on the lawn outside pub's side entrance, Sibby couldn't help but admire the way the evening sun lit up just the tops of the mountains on the other side of the loch. Ollie drew closer and pointed out the slash in the mountain that was the old limestone quarry above Marble Mountain village. His description was, however, lost beneath the thunderous rumble of that camouflage pickup truck Sibby had seen a few days before. Ollie waved to the driver out of habit.

"Camouflaged, from what?" Sibby wondered aloud.

"Kind of stands out, doesn't it," chuckled Ollie. "But that's the point, I think. In an area where every man drives either a black Dodge Ram or a red dump truck, the camouflage makes him stand out!"

"As if the noise isn't enough," she pointed out.

"Something bigger, badder and bolder will come along one day."

Sibby wondered how Ollie had learned to fit in here, and wondered if she wasn't too far removed to even understand it. They rounded a hedge and made for the parking lot to the rear of the hotel. Ollie stopped suddenly.

"I almost forgot," he hurried. "John-Duncan told me to tell you that you might want to talk to Sander MacDonald. You can usually find him in his Kempt Road garage."

"Is that near here? I'm on my way up to Sydney in the morning."

"Down."

"Down?" asked Sibby, visualizing her road map, which clearly showed that Sydney was up in the northeast corner of Cape Breton.

"Up to Halifax, down to Sydney," Ollie explained.

"Down," she repeated doubtfully. Is it even possible to get used to this place?

"Yes. Halifax is upwind, Sydney down."

"You've got to be kidding," Sibby raised one eyebrow. "So, you were about to point me to Kempt Road."

"Yes. Go left from here, and take your first left onto Black River Road to the end. Turn right on old route 4. I think Sander's about 5 k from the intersection." Then he added, "will you be around for a few days yet? I could show you more of the area. Kind of nice to have fresh ears about."

"I'm not sure," Sibby replied. She'd had a fleeting thought that she might take the time to get to know the area better, and maybe Olaf Balderston too. 'Get a grip,' she said to herself. 'This is not a novel.'

"So, Kempt Road," she affirmed.

"Yes, about 5 kilometres from the intersection."

"On Kempt Road."

"In. Kempt Road isn't a road, it's a place."

∞∞

'Any way you look at it,' Sibby mused, 'Cape Breton is – what did he say? a place apart? It's that and more,' she thought as the fall landscape parted before the bow of her bright yellow and green kayak.

She checked, for about the two hundredth time, the taut nylon ropes straining against the early morning autumn air. If she didn't take too many breaks, she thought, she'd surely reach her destination in late afternoon.

Not long ago such a distance would have seemed unreasonable, given her perceived level of fitness, not to mention the unknowns that had lay ahead.

'Motivation is a powerful drug,' she thought. 'It can point you in unexpected directions.'

Sibby had learned something about herself through her voyage to the unknown in search of who-knows-what. Perhaps her mother knew as much when she made her promise to seek out her ancestors.

"There's no place like home, Toto," she mused as her car merged with I-95 traffic on the outskirts of Bangor she laughed at herself for addressing the twin rock paintings tucked away in her suitcase. "There's no place like home."

fin

RYAN'S BELT

"**I**t was something Frank said."

"Frank?" I wondered if they could hear the tremor in my voice.

"What was it you said, Frank? About the garden, Frank? Frank said it would be nice for you to fix up Papa's old garden. Enjoy some flowers, maybe grow some vegt'bles."

My ever-thoughtful sister-in-law, Rose.

∞∞

Rose and her husband Frank, my only sibling, enjoyed a garden showcase of green-thumbery in their suburban neighbourhood in Brampton, west of Toronto. It's brilliant in the pictures. I've never actually seen it, having never been to their house. Not that I'd have gone all the way to Ontario to see them. No need. They spend their entire summers here.

Why they have such an elaborate garden, when they spent the summers 2,000 km away, here on Cape Breton Island was beyond my ken. Two-thousand-one-hundred-three-point-seven-kilometres, I should say – as Rose would – from their back yard to mine, where Rose, my brother, their children and their dog, Alexander Keats, year after year spent almost their entire summer vacation. Their children, now grown and with families of their own, no longer make the trip. But Frank and Rose and the dog do. Their entire. Long. Hot. Summer. Vacation. *Their* vacation.

But, as I keep reminding myself, Frank is my only sibling, and this was our childhood home, our parents' home – and our father's father's. Now it's my home. His family is my family, so my home is their home.

Family is important to Cape Bretoners, Capers some call us, which is especially evident in summer. If you happen to drive through our village, The Landing, during the first week of August in any given year, you'd be forgiven for thinking there's been a natural disaster. During old home week, every front yard, back yard, field and gravel pit from here to Malagawatch is a patchwork of tents, trailers and motorhomes. Every kitchen table is reconfigured by a sheet of plywood to accommodate visiting relatives from Ottawa to Oshawa, from Winnipeg to Walla Walla.

My brother's seniority at the tractor factory in Brampton means that their old home week is just about all summer long: three weeks vacation on either side of the factory's annual two-week shutdown. Eight glorious weeks in their classic seven-metre blue-and-cream-coloured, third-hand travel trailer in my backyard. Eight weeks to "excape the heat and humility of the city, in God's country," is how Rose puts it. She's the educated one of the pair. I can't help but note the ironic play on her missed pronunciation – for indeed she and Frank are ex Capers.

Frank left school in grade eight. After years of underemployment and underachievement on our farm, Rose's brother got him a job sweeping floors at the factory. Rose soon followed, lured by the prospects of marriage, children and a prosperous life in the big city.

Cape Breton is God's country, and God's country is Cape Breton, people say. Well, God has either a sense of humour or a mean streak. I don't recall the former being preached but the latter is pretty evident in the Bible and it's put into practice in Cape Breton. Make no mistake, it's beautiful here – rugged coastline, verdant glens brilliant in autumn are balanced bitterly by winter, which I guess is evidence of the mean streak. Don't get me going about spring. Lack of it, that is.

Anyway, summer can be brutally hot in southern Ontario, so expat Cape Bretoners flock to the seacoast of their fledging. Here they spend no small measure of time lording it over us poor relatives stuck in God's country, and reminding us of the benefits of living in Ontario. Behind our backs our late father – my and Frank's father – spent the summer rolling his eyes skyward.

To keep the peace, our mother used to shoo him out of doors to tend his little garden patch – the retirement corner of their modest farm – "for some peas and quiet," Rose often punned. There's a photo of him taken the year before he died hanging in the kitchen next to the china cabinet – the picture, that is, not our father. It was taken at sunset, his tanned face contrasting his mane of white hair in the orange glow of an August evening.

"I always loved that pitcher," Rose often sighed. "He just looks so ... so ... extinguished, don't you think? I loved him like a father." The photograph was my reminder of how reluctant father was to return from his garden to the light of the kitchen at the end of the day – to return to the slurping of tea, smacking of biscuits drowned in molasses and the coaxing of us all into one last hand of Rummoli before bed. Both our parents have gone to their reward now; father's garden was allowed to grow over.

Expat – expatriate – is the accepted term for people who relocate to another country. Rose says the word really applies to Cape Bretoners because they are extremely patriotic, no matter that so many live and work at good-paying jobs in Canada's industrial centres.

Frank and Rose live in a fairly large split-level house with a finished basement in one of the endless tangles of residential streets in Brampton – paved driveway, attached garage full of tools, bordered by a mature but dishevelled hedge. Out back, their yard is of lush, green, mowable grass – except for the little bleached patches where their dog, Alexander Keats, shits whatever is left of the radioactive canine caviar their big-city vet has recommended.

The grass in their pictures in no way resembles whatever is growing around the majority of houses in The Landing. That goes for my yard too, which, as I started to say, their third-hand travel trailer occupied for two months every summer, and under which Alexander Keats was chained in refuge from all the elements the skies over Loch Bras d'Or are capable of delivering.

∞∞

Once in a while, if the night sky was clear, Rose would invite me to bring a six-pack and to join them under the stars, to bask in the blue light of the television they had hooked up to my satellite dish to watch "*Carnation St*" or maybe "*Downtown Alley.*"

Sometimes, during commercials, Rose, the ever gracious host – who was educated, she liked to remind Frank – would ponder the stunning starscape and, with a majestic sweep of her can of beer, mispronounce the glories of the constellations.

"See the Big Tipper?" she quizzed one night. "That grouping of seven stars like a ladle and handle kind of tipped over. It's also known as the Great Bear, did you know that? Ursula Major. The Natives called it Moon. They had legends about the constellations."

She got that almost right. The Mi'kmaq know it as Muin, not Moon. Indeed, they have an elaborate legend detailing its seasonal traverse of the night sky.

"And there's the Littler Tipper. And see that zig-zag one, like the outline of a chair? That's Cassie's peeing chair."

"Cassiopeia," I corrected. "Cassiopeia's Chair."

"Chair, or toilet," blurted Frank in a rare flash of humour. He got to his feet and headed around the trailer for the house. "I gotta go use Cassie's chair," he chuckled over his shoulder.

Rose continued. "And that one – see the three bright stars in a row? That's Ryan's Belt."

"Ryan's Belt?" I repeated. "Orion's Belt maybe?"

"O'Ryan. Right. And that's his sword."

I couldn't see it. Then again, neither could she. Orion is not in our night sky until September. She was looking at Draco. In her defence, I've heard others make the same error.

∞∞

About the third or fourth week of last summer's vacation, I ventured out to trim the weeds that formed a low hedge around the trailer, hiding Alexander Keats and God-knows-what from the view from my kitchen window. Four times a day in summer, I faced that view while washing dishes, turning my back to the lingering conversation at the table, to try to glimpse the sunset.

Lingering is the best way to put it, for it was the same as the last conversation – and the one before that, and before that – the one which details all the haves they have and all the have-nots we have not. It's absurd to me that they drone on about all they have up there, while sitting at the kitchen table down here.

This particular day, lost as I was in the noise of the electric trimmer, I rounded the corner of the trailer only to bang my head on the aluminum frame of their fully extended awning. It was only a glancing blow, but it elicited a little curse – a curse I repeated absentmindedly when I refocused my attention on the scene in front of me. Lost to me in the noise, Frank and Rose were stretched out in newly purchased his-and-hers *chaises longues* –"shade lounges," Rose called them – looking a little sheepish at hearing my off-colour outburst.

Letting the trimmer go silent, I apologized for the interruption – damn ingrained Cape Breton manners.

"Aw, you spoilt our surprise," Rose said with a playful look of hurt.

"Surprise?" Did that come out right? I was doing maintenance around *their* trailer in *my* yard, only to be told I 'spoilt their surprise,' but I let it go. As always.

"Yes," said Rose. "It was Frank's idea. To surprise you. I *told* him you don't like surprises.

"Franks' idea?" I asked.

"It was something Frank said about Papa's garden. We wanted to surprise you."

"Garden?" I turned to follow their eyes and their meaning just in case I had heard wrong.

"So you can relax," Frank said reassuringly. Through the weeds under the trailer, Alexander Keats swished his tail in approval.

"You should have a garden," beamed Rose. "Like your father. Where you can get away from it all."

'Apparently not,' I said to myself. Then aloud, "I-I don't know what to say."

Well, I knew what to say, I just wouldn't say it. Some years ago, as I mentioned, we had a garden. Rather, our father had a garden, but I had decided that a garden was too much work and had let it grow over.

"It was all overgrowed," Frank admonished. I preferred to think of it as providing habitat for small birds and bugs and God-knows-what.

"Just too busy, I guess," I excused.

"We wanted to fix it up. You should see our garden at home," Rose beamed.

To myself I thought, 'No, YOU should see more of your garden at home.'

"It will bring you peas and harmony," Rose said, resurrecting her little pun.

From Frank's hands came the 'phsst' of a fresh can of Keith's. He was standing in the doorway of the trailer, surveying their endeavour.

"You can see it better up here," he invited.

"Take it all in, girl. We're not going anywhere." Rose's words bounced from one side of my head to the other – 'Not. Going. Anywhere, she'd said.'

Where the area once known as father's garden – my backyard nature trust – had been uniformly overgrown with flowering weeds and hay, now resembled a toddler's attempt at a doll's haircut.

A path had been beaten down the middle. Three or four metres in was a sizeable patch of withered grasses and weeds, possibly explaining the strong smell of vinegar in the air. To one side there was a pile of rocks, rocks that were quite uniform, giving rise to a pang of anxiety as I wondered where they came from.

"I'm thinking, 'rock garden'," Frank said with another wave of his Keith's. "No mowing rocks."

"We know how much you hate mowing," Rose said pointedly, with a subtle tip of her head toward the unkempt lawn surrounding their trailer.

"It'll be a rough outline of the night sky," said Frank, puffing up dramatically.

"Like astrology," said Rose. "We'll make a little night sky rock garden. Your own little Stonehinge."

"Kind of," Frank said helpfully.

I wondered to myself what was the latest in suburban gardens up where they live the rest of the year. As if to answer, Frank reported that he'd seen rock gardens "on the garden TV." He reached into the trailer and took a crumpled piece of paper from the counter.

Smoothing out the wrinkles, he waved it in front of me. "We made a sketch."

"Looks like the stars," I ventured.

"You could add a percolator for a bit of shade," Rose offered. "If you wanted."

"It would go there." Frank pointed to his drawing, where the outlines of rocks of various sizes and colours formed a small square in one gravelly corner of what I can only describe as a maze, like the ones you see in puzzle books – connect-the-dots for pre-schoolers.

My head was spinning just a little, perhaps from the collision with the canopy, but more likely from worlds colliding. I lowered myself from the step, focusing my eyes on my feet for assurance and balance.

"We didn't get around to plant planets yet." Rose made a sweeping motion with her Keith's.

"But more rocks than plants," Frank promised.

I followed his gaze to the pile of dried grass and weeds that had once covered the little area of dirt now envisioned as a model of the heavens. How did I not see all this going on in my own backyard, my quiet little corner of the universe?

"Stop there, Frank," I blurted. "Let me think."

"This kind of garden needs no maintenance," Frank promised. "No grass to upkeep."

"It's the latest thing," said Rose. "It's very European," she added, "or Japanese."

"No grass to mow," she repeated as my eyes traced the outline of grass and weeds growing tall in the shaded outline of their trailer. In my mind's eye, I could visualize the area as it once was, a uniform savanna separating me from the jungle that was once our father's escape. 'Where,' I wondered, 'could I escape?'

∞∞

"Frank is thinking of retiring," Rose said at supper a few evenings later. "We can work on the garden together then." I swear, my head spun completely around.

Of course, nothing had happened to the "garden" since they showed me their plans. Not that I encouraged them. I didn't *want* anything to happen. I wanted my yard back. I wanted my view of the setting sun gilding the perennial weeds and hay, or whatever that was.

"I don't want a garden," I blurted, feeling flushed. Seeing the way my words stopped them mid fork, I almost said 'sorry.' Almost.

"I don't want a garden," I repeated more calmly.

"But you need a garden," stated Frank. "Our father's garden."

As he was the boy of the family, I had deferred to Frank my entire life, even after he left and got married, and even after I moved back home to look after our aging parents. Even after they were gone I felt forced, out of family loyalty, to defer to him – and to Rose.

"Rock gardens are the perfect co-promise," offered Rose, "and they're the latest thing. You may not know the difference, but others will appreciate—"

"This has to stop," I interupted shakily.

"I mean it. This has to stop," I hoped I was speaking more firmly than it felt.

"If you're going to be like that, we can forget the garden for this year," Frank offered weakly.

"No. This." I gestured all inclusively – the kitchen table, the kitchen at large, the dirty dishes, the back-yard, the trailer. "*This* has to stop."

∞∞

During the night, it was not unusual to hear one of them creeping around inside the house, whether coming in to the bathroom or the fridge, and that night was no different. What *was* different, however, was the quiet come morning. When I opened the bathroom window curtains after my shower, I was struck by the unobstructed view of the fields behind the house, a trailerless view.

It was gone. They were gone. Like 'sheeps pissing in the night,' Rose once said about their travels. They had broken camp and moved on without a goodbye – in their wake a patch of dead grass, a dozen empty vinegar jugs, an outline of weeds and forty-or-fifty little piles of dog shit. Poor Frank. Poor Alexander Keats.

∞∞

The next summer I did, in fact, create a rock garden. It was more modest than Frank and Rose had in mind, just a two-and-a-half by seven metres dead zone, bordered by a strip of rich green grass, like an outline of an abandoned homestead. The rocks in my little garden were not aligned with the stars, but I did feel that the stars were favourably aligned. Rose was right; it was very uplifting.

fin

POOR WOOLLY'S
HALLMARK CHRISTMAS

Poor Woolly had been changing TV channels to find the news, having finished watching *Jeopardy!*, when he glimpsed her. He got quite agitated when he couldn't figure out on which channel she'd been.

He couldn't get the regular TV signal in his modest cabin in a corner of the old farm where he grew up. After both his parents passed – first his father, then his mother – his sister bought him "The Dish," as everyone calls it, as an early Christmas present. 'So he wouldn't feel so lonely up there,' she'd said, even though it was her idea that he move out of the house they'd grown up in. She thought it was too big for just one person.

He was quite comfortable in his two-room cabin. It didn't have all the comforts of his growing-up home, like his mother's prized China or the family pictures that had cluttered the parlour. He had all he needed when the TV was on.

When they were still alive, his parents had allowed him to watch the news and any other show he wanted, but only for one hour a day other than the news. They didn't really approve of television at all but granted it in measured doses because they recognized it as part of modernity. And it directed Poor Woolly's attention elsewhere than them, if only for a couple of hours.

He finds the constancy of TV upsetting. He prefers books and newspapers for their linearity. He can take his time. During the day he is entertained by the birds and other animals who live and die around his cabin. In the evening he reads and watches his two hours of television.

The cabin boasts little by way of amenities – two small tables, one he uses as a kitchen table and one under the television in a corner of the kitchen. There are two chairs, including the one he sits on at the kitchen table. 'Minimalist,' his sister calls it. He spends most of his time in the kitchen – a primitive version of open plan, as TV designers call it. The kitchen is where the wood stove is and where he sleeps on a cot in winter. In summer he sleeps in his bunk – not much more than a board and a blanket, really – in the other room.

At the foot of his bunk squats an old trunk full of things his sister didn't want, but things he did want – extra things, memories, including a picture of his grandfather. His sister had taken most of the old pictures to her house in the city, where she and her family could enjoy them.

Poor Woolly understood. The pictures saved her a lot of time and travel because she didn't have to actually visit "home"; it was always right there on her walls.

∞∞

Born William MacAulay, the name Willie suited him better as a lad. People around here pronounce that more like Wullie, which morphed to Woolly, on account of his thick and wiry hair. Poor Woolly is not too swift, some say, lacking wit, some say. Woolly headed, they say. His conversational style is off-putting to those who make too much of talking and not enough of listening.

Most regard him as a bit addled, if not downright slow, and he's treated as such by most, in that demeaning way that busy people have. You know, that little shake of the head and double-click of the tongue – 'tsk-tsk, poor Woolly.' Everyone in The Landing has referred to him as Poor Woolly for so long that he answers to it.

Poor Woolly had been slow getting the hang of his new television. Even with all the channels he could possibly want, he still watched in measured amounts. One December evening when switching channels, he saw *her* on *his* television.

Was he dreaming? "Blair?" he cried aloud. "Blair?"

That was how he knew her – Blair Warner, the highfalutin teenage socialite on a television show from a long time ago. *The Facts of Life.* He watched that show many times as a youngster. He often chose it for some of his allowable entertainment time. He had a crush on Blair Warner.

Now she was on the Hallmark Channel, he determined, once he found it, and it was a Christmas story – not *the* Christmas story, mind you. He hadn't seen the start but determined it was about one pretty woman, Blair Warner, and a handsome man who didn't seem to like each other at first. They got caught in a snowstorm, saved Christmas for orphans, fell in love, had a fight and fell in love again.

He just had to watch the rest of the movie on account of still being head-over-heels for Blair Warner – which was a bit of a problem because he went over his TV time limit and would have to make it up by skipping tomorrow's news or *Jeopardy!* At the end of the movie he learned that her real name is Lisa Whelchel, and the movie was called *Christmas Comes to St. Agnes's.*

The last Christmas shows he had seen on TV were while his parents were both alive, usually starring Cape

Breton singer Rita MacNeil, or the Cape Breton Celtic band the Barra MacNeils, or Rita MacNeil AND the Barra MacNeils. Those MacNeils sure love Christmas.

There was no Scotch music at St. Agnes's orphanage in the movie, but that didn't matter to Poor Woolly. Blair Warner was in it. Blair in front of a big red barn lit up with strings of white lights and gigantic red bows. Blair decorating for Christmas in the general store. Blair making gingerbread houses at the orphanage. Blair and the handsome man kissing under the mistletoe. Poor Woolly usually covered his eyes when confronted with that much drama, but this time he couldn't taken his eyes off the screen for more than an hour.

He watched more TV movies that Christmas than in his entire previous life. And he enjoyed them. No violence. No bad guys. Just happy, clean-shaven, predictable people with good manners and good teeth. It was very comforting. And addictive, though he did not see another one starring Lisa Welchel, his Blair Warner. Christmas came and went. The movies stopped. Life returned to normal.

∞∞

More important to our story, winter passed too, then spring – such as spring is in Cape Breton – then it was summer. Poor Woolly's life was more orderly in summer. More predictable. He knew what he'd be doing every day, especially Tuesdays, and he liked it that way. This year, however, August had a few surprises. He did not like surprises.

Poor Woolly prided himself on keeping abreast of world events and the comings and goings in and out of The Landing for much of his adult life. There were times, of course, that he felt he had missed something significant – anyone would – like Rip van Winkle waking in the land of the Lilliputians. (Poor Woolly is well read, but he sometimes mashes up his references.)

One time he got the dates mixed up between the annual gospel tent and the annual beer tent. Anyone could make the same mistake – both events used the same marquis tent, just on different dates.

When Poor Woolly realized his mistake and got up to leave, Brother Love thought he was coming forward to be saved, and made a big fuss over him. Not wishing to disrespect or disappoint the preacher, Poor Woolly passed the collection plate when he was asked. In his nervousness, when he finished the back row he kept right on going out the back of the tent – collection plate and all. Anyone could have made the same mistake.

He knows everyone in The Landing, and everyone knows him, but when he came down the hill that one Tuesday in August – like he did every Tuesday and again on cheque day if it didn't fall on a Tuesday – Poor Woolly thought he'd taken a wrong turn. He was only somewhat reassured when he spied Mayor Bossy headed his way at a pace that belied her physique.

The Landing doesn't have a real mayor, nor does it need or want one. Still, each generation has its community character who acts like they own the place. Bessy MacGillivray is this generation's unofficial mayor. Everyone knows her as Bossy.

Bossy must have seen him coming because she met him at the crossroads – all out of breath and dishevelled from the effort. She told him, her voice barely above a whisper, "today is not a good day, Woolly." Looking past her, Poor Woolly could see for himself that this was no ordinary Tuesday. Lining both sides of the main road through town was a forest of movie lights, cameras and activities. No wonder Bossy was on edge.

It was true that she had been uncharacteristically chipper of late, grinning ear-to-ear and dressed to the nines, like she was getting married again. Today she had on so much makeup you could barely make out the scars below her left eye which she'd sustained in an argument with a racoon.

The Landing was dressed to the nines as well – you'd hardly recognize the place for new signs on buildings that hadn't housed businesses in years, and on false storefront facades erected on vacant lots. It was like the village of old in the yellowed photographs that used to hang in his mother's parlour, now in his sister's house in the city, save for the one in his trunk. That was the picture of his grandfather, all dressed up and holding the reins of his champion carriage horse. Poor Woolly hadn't really missed that picture but seeing it brought to life like that he suddenly did.

"It's Tuesday," he reminded Mayor Bossy. "On Tuesday I go to town and get my mail and the newspaper and visit with Kenzie because he got my groceries yesterday – Kenzie goes to town for groceries on Monday, for the bargains, I feed the ducks on Monday. Monday they had an election in Brazil, a man who hates monkeys is president now; there was a police raid in Lexington, guns and drugs, drugs and guns. They said it was going to rain tomorrow. I don't like to be in the rain, but I see snow on the ground. How can there be snow on the ground? In summer, the air is hot and it is going to rain but there is snow – it's Tuesday."

Accustomed to being cut short, Woolly's intense oral deliveries crammed as many topics into as little time as possible. It was as though his thoughts were on little scraps of paper in a jar from which he drew at random, hardly taking a breath in between.

"Yes, yes, I know Woolly," Mayor Bossy told him. "But this Tuesday is different. They are making a movie.

A Christmas movie. Here." She paused, spreading her arms as though giving a benediction. "In The Landing. For television."

"On a Tuesday," Poor Woolly confirmed.

"Yes, on a Tuesday," she consoled.

"And it's Christmas." Poor Woolly pointed to a small pile of snow at the corner. There was more snow in more little piles along the street.

"It's a Christmas movie," he confirmed. "I watched Christmas movies last Christmas. One with Blair Warner. She saved the orphans' Christmas. There were more but none with Rita MacNeil. She died. They put her in a teapot. My sister sends me socks for Christmas. And fruitcake. My mother made fruitcake. I like gravy on my turkey. No fruitcake in August."

"Pretend Christmas," Mayor Bossy assured him. *"Christmas in Kensington."*

Poor Woolly shuffled his feet as he thought about this. Bossy manoeuvered her considerable self as if to block him, should he make a break for it and perhaps break something or get in the way of her possible discovery as an actor.

"It's Tuesday. On Tuesday I—"

"I know it's Tuesday, Woolly. We're making a movie—"

"A Christmas movie," he pointed out. "But it's not Christmas. It's T—"

"Would you like to watch them make the movie?" Mayor Bossy gently slid her hand under Poor Woolly's elbow in a bid to both comfort and guide him. "We can watch from over at the post office."

Sensing he was wary of the pile of snow on the Post office porch, Mayor Bossy pointed and told him again, "it's pretend snow, Woolly, for pretend Christmas."

"Poor Woolly," he reminded her.

From their new vantage point, Poor Woolly could now see small groups of people gathered around various equipment, intent on small televisions, banks of lighting or, lastly, a table laden with a big silver urn with a sign that said "coffee," next to boxes overflowing with donuts and sandwiches and trays of vegetables.

"People here drink tea," Poor Woolly noted aloud.

Away from the cameras and activity, sleek motorhomes and a purple bus peeked out from behind pretend houses and stores. There was such a tangle of wires and cables strewn about the village it looked to Poor Woolly like mating season in the Sargasso Sea. He became aware of the throaty hum of a chorus of generators. Their resonance rattled in his chest like their current was passing through him. It was not a pleasant feeling.

The streetscape also had Poor Woolly rattled – a streetscape that he knew from pictures and stories, but not for real. He was standing on the porch of the same old post office, his post office, but next door in the empty lot now stood MacPhie's old mill, two sides of it anyway. On the side facing the road churned a gigantic water wheel, just like in an old picture at Kenzie's house.

A short distance away was the old carriage factory – just like in the pictures – around which a group of young people in old clothes were standing, talking, drinking tea and puffing on strangely pungent smokes. Above them a large painted sign said: "MacPhie Carriage Makers." Behind them, young men in jeans and soiled T-shirts were fussing over unseen details, moving this wagon here, that horse there. "But MacPhie's is only in pictures," remarked Poor Woolly in consternation.

Across the road was the old tannery from the pictures. Over the porch, a sign advertised "Hector MacLean, Shoemaker – Leather Goods Bought and

Sold," like in the pictures. An old man, who didn't really look all that old, was getting his hair combed by a young woman in a halter-top and tights. A team of horses stood outside MacDonald's Mercantile – just like in his mother's pictures – their flanks and tails twitching under the assault of flies. Poor Woolly knows a thing or two about horses.

"Those are Joe MacInnis's horses," he said aloud to no one in particular. "That's Joe MacInnis's rig. Joe MacInnis lets me ride in that wagon sometimes. Sally, Betty, Angela and Rosie. Joe MacInnis's horses. Joe MacInnis must be in the store, but the store is only in pictures. The MacInnises came from Scotland, from Lewis. The MacDonalds came from Scotland too, we all came from Scotland. Scotland wants to be independent. England wants to leave Europe. Those are Joe MacInnis's real horses, not pretend."

There was a sudden burst of activity in front of the tannery which pricked up the horses' ears and sparked Mayor Bossy into action.

"I have to be going now," she told him while making an unnecessary adjustment to her blouse. "Maybe you should think about heading home?"

"I always talk to Kenzie on Tuesday. Kenzie has my tea and my eggs. I should talk to Kenzie before I go."

"Kenzie's tied up with the movie too, Woolly. Almost everyone has a little job with the movie. I don't think you will be seeing him today."

"Everybody's tied up," he repeated. "Tied up with the movie. With pretend Christmas. With pretend snow. With Joe MacInnis's horses. Percherons. Joe MacInnis's horses are P—"

"Yes, yes, Woolly," Mayor Bossy dismissed. "Now run along home, so you don't get in the way."

"Poor Woolly," he corrected.

Bossy started to walk away but stopped, as though regretting her dismissive behaviour. Poor Woolly was a lovable local character for whom everyone had time unless they didn't.

"I'm sorry, Woolly. It's just—" she stretched out her arms in a grand gesture. "A *mooo-vie!*" she emphasized, looking at him half apologetic, half appealing. "It's not every day someone makes a Christmas mooo-vie in The Landing."

"Pretend Christmas."

"Right. But a real movie. They will be here for a few weeks, bringing a lot of business to the village, and people will see the movie and want to come to visit and spend money, and—"

"Pretend money?" asked Poor Woolly.

"Real money," she answered. "And other TV shows might come."

"No stores." Poor Woolly pointed across the street. "Those are pretend stores. You can only spend pretend money in a pretend store. You need real stores for real money. No stores in The Landing anymore."

Mayor Bossy looked at the man quizzically and she might have responded had he not interrupted.

"How long will they pretend it's Christmas?"

"A few weeks. When you next come to get your mail—"

"Tuesday."

"Tuesday," she continued, "be sure to not get in the way of the cameras, okay? Look! There's Stacey Vibert, the TV star. She's in the movie. Have you seen Stacey Vibert on TV Woolly?"

"I saw Rita MacNeil on TV." 'And Blair Warner,' he quietly added to himself.

Poor Woolly watched the proceedings a little while longer. Actors, men and women, did their thing for the cameras for a minute or two, then stopped, then repeated. It seemed to him that they spent more time not acting.

"It's a good thing it's pretend snow," he mused as he stepped onto the road and – after pausing to get his bearings – headed to the crossroads and the walk home. "Stacey Vibert is so thin she would freeze if it was real Christmas."

∞∞

On Tuesday next, Poor Woolly headed to the village a little more slowly than usual. It wasn't that he dreaded the expected disruption of his routine, but he was understandably nervous about what might greet him.

This time, there was no sign of Mayor Bossy. Poor Woolly didn't know if that was a good thing or bad. Sometimes he found her rather pushy and dismissive, but at least she conversed with him – in a manner of speaking.

With hardly a glance up the street, he entered the post office to collect his mail, and perhaps a little something from the candy dish on the counter. The postmaster, Joanie, always has a dish of people candy and a dish of dog candy ready. She was on the phone. He waited for her to finish and get his mail, quietly swaying back and forth, back and forth, left to right.

"Good morning Woolly." Joanie smiled as she went quickly in and out of the back room, a few pieces of mail, flyers and a newspaper bound by a bit of ribbon tied in a colourful bow just for him.

"Good morning Joanie." Poor Woolly reached for his mail with his right hand and for the candy dish with his left, but the manoeuvre was suddenly aborted when he spied the candy assortment. Puzzled, Joanie set his bundle of mail on the counter and waited a moment before encouraging him to take a candy.

"Help yourself," she said. "They're some of your favourites."

"Christmas candy?" he asked. Glancing at the calendar on the wall he added, "it's August."

"In honour of the movies, Woolly. Christmas candy. A little joke." She laughed. "Christmas in August."

"Pretend Christmas," he reminded her.

"The candies are real," she promised as she fussed with the dish a little.

That was good enough for Poor Woolly. Joanie is a good soul and someone he trusts. She treats him like she does everyone, never talking down to him or ignoring him. He reviewed the contents of the dish slowly, as though he could see through the brightly coloured wrappers before choosing his favourite.

"Did you see them making the movie, Woolly?" Joanie asked.

"Yes. *Christmas in Kensington*. Stacey Vibert. Pretend snow, pretend stores, pretend Christmas. The pretend president wants a real wall. The ER is closed again this week, don't get sick, don't get hurt. It hasn't rained in a week. Too dry. No bees when it's too dry. Too dusty."

"*Christmas on Owl Mountain*, Woolly. It's *Christmas on Owl Mountain*."

He was sure Mayor Bossy told him pretend Christmas was in pretend Kensington.

Sensing his confusion, Joanie explained. "They're making more than one movie, Woolly. Three, I think."

Poor Woolly looked over Joanie's shoulder and through the window where last week there was a pretend mill. Only it wasn't a pretend mill anymore, it was ... what was it? Poor Woolly studied the view while he unwrapped his candy. A big house all decorated for Christmas. The pretend mill was gone, and in its place, a pretend house.

"Quality Street," he said suddenly.

"What's that?" Joanie looked up from her computer.

"Quality Street. The candies. My favourite. The old mill looked like a picture puzzle. That doesn't look like a real house. This is not Owl Mountain. It's MacIntosh Mountain. Marble Mountain. Sporting Mountain."

"Wait until you see what they did to MacPhie's, Woolly." Joanie was half turned toward the window and looking farther up the road. "Done over for a Christmas dance."

"Pretend Christmas," he corrected.

"Pretend Christmas," she agreed. "Oh, look. They're taking a break. Quick now, this would be a good time to go along the street and see what they've done to The Landing for the movie."

Poor Woolly wasn't too sure about that, but his friend Kenzie lived at the far end of the village, and if he wanted his milk and eggs, he would have to leave the safety of the post office. He cracked open the front door, being careful not to bump into anyone who might be about to come in. Pushing it wide, he stepped fully through – just as a plume of fake snow landed at his feet. It was sprayed from a gigantic fan mounted on the back of a slowly passing pick-up truck.

The look on Poor Woolly's face must have betrayed his great surprise and confusion, because the man behind the snow fan let out a booming guffaw, momentarily losing control of his weapon causing the plume of snow to bury Poor Woolly's feet to a shovelable depth. The man quickly yelled an apologetic "sorry buddy!" before continuing his snowy mission up the road.

The fake snow had the positive secondary effect of dampening the dusty street. It had been paved, but only once, and that was many years ago. It was a dirt road now, the result of a nasty turn in local politics when Mayor Bossy lost an argument with a Tory Transportation Minister. Bossy told him that our roads were so broken up and full of potholes the government might as well tear up the asphalt. A dirt road could be maintained by anyone with a garden tractor, she'd said. The Minister, in a fit of rhetorical belligerence, agreed and made it happen. People in The Landing are just waiting for a change of government to get back on the paving list. Should only be another thirty years, they say.

The snow truck and that crisis having passed, Poor Woolly nervously looked across the road to see if anyone had witnessed his embarrassment. When his eyes fell on the one person who did, his jaw dropped in recognition and disbelief. Blair Warner. In the flesh. In his village. Or rather, in the pretend village from the old pictures. She was sitting on a bench on the veranda of the Owl Mountain Credit Union, right across from the post office. Only there is no credit union for real, just a pretend one – and just the face of it.

The bench was real, and the veranda was real, and— 'oh my,' he thought. 'What if she is not real?' Or maybe it wasn't really her at all. *The Facts of Life* was, what, thirty years ago? Forty? She'd be, what, fifty? Fifty-five? But he knew in his heart it was her. He could feel it. He'd know her anywhere. Anywhere! But was she real? Was the real Blair here, in The Landing?

Poor Woolly shook off the pretend snow, instinctively stomping his feet like it was January. Hearing him, Lisa Whelchel – his Blair – looked up from across the road. Poor Woolly stopped in mid stomp, frozen like it really was January; a frozen grin cracked his face from ear to ear.

Recognizing the situation, not the person, Blair – Lisa – gave a friendly little wave and a smile, which Poor Woolly took for permission to not only wave back but to leave the post office steps and head toward her. Sensing what was coming, the star's look of affirmation turned quickly to a frown of concentration, and she looked down at her papers with determination.

Poor Woolly had seen that look many times, and he abandoned the thought of engaging with her. Instead, he turned abruptly up the road, intending to resume his errands and go to Kenzie's for tea. He had to pick up the groceries his friend should have for him. To get there, he would have to run the gauntlet of cameras, cables and cast members milling about on their break.

Normally, he would have a shy smile and a nod for each of them if they caught his eye, but he was mortified by his faux-pas with Blair, and he passed solemnly through the crowds – well, crowds by local standards. Hurriedly, if awkwardly, his eyes focused straight ahead, leaving his feet to fend for themselves as he went. Poor Woolly was the picture of determination, and people instinctively stepped aside or backward as he passed, causing him to feel very much alone.

∞∞

Thankfully Kenzie was home, though it was earlier than usual. On familiar ground once more, Poor Woolly let down his guard and fairly burst, his thoughts bubbling over.

"Blair Warner is in The Landing. She is a hundred years old. The movie. The movie is a hundred. Not the movie, just the buildings. Christmas in July. Pretend Christmas. How do they make it snow in July? Pretend snow doesn't melt! Not *Christmas in Cape Breton*, the movie. Not *Christmas in Kensington. Christmas on Owl Mountain.* She smiled at me."

Kenzie did his best to normalize the situation for Poor Woolly, telling him it was just a movie and just for a few weeks.

"Movies," Poor Woolly countered. "Bossy says more movies. Joanie says three movies. It's confusing."

"It is a little confusing, Woolly. They make several at the same time – at least, in the same place one after another to save money. They just change things slightly to make it look different for a different story. Even have the same extras. Just dress them up."

Slowly at first, then quickening, recognition washed over Poor Woolly. Last winter he had watched a movie almost every week hoping to see Blair again. There *was* something about the movies that had troubled him, but in his quest for her, he hadn't registered what that was. The stories were different – and at the same time similar – and the stars were different, though he saw the actor he now knew was Stacey Vibert in three of them. Many of the towns and villages and buildings were alike – at the same time not. He was sure now that most of the buildings in most of the movies were the same.

When he thought about it, he remembered that more of the people were the same too, like Kenzie said.

"Were you in a movie, Kenzie? I didn't see you on TV. Were you extra? No one is extra. Ma told us everyone is special. No one is special. Everyone has gifts. Everyone has a place. No one is extra. Ma told—"

"They hire extras for the movies Woolly. They pay you to just stand around or pretend to shop while the famous ones talk and act. Top dollar for doin' nothin'. Quite the racket."

∞∞

Poor Woolly went into The Landing only on Tuesdays, except for cheque day if that didn't fall on a Tuesday. But for the first time in two decades, give or take, he went into the village on a Wednesday, and he was dressed to the nines for the occasion – 1909.

The day before, after Kenzie drove him home, Poor Woolly made his supper in a distracted silence that lasted through the evening, followed by a restless night. He wasn't so much troubled as bewildered by Tuesday's events.

He must have slept some, because he awoke with a start as though someone had turned on a light before dawn. It was him, actually, fully engaged in the memories in the trunk at the foot of the bunk. Two hours later he was on his way to The Landing, even though it was Wednesday.

When he rounded the turn by the church, he could see that the village was already alive with activity. Crews were busily reeling out thick black cables and struggling with arrays of lights atop flimsy poles mounted on skinny wheels that rattled annoyingly on the dirt road.

As he got near the post office, he could see young people opening and closing white and silver umbrellas – even though there wasn't a cloud in the sky   and scrambling up and down ladders adjusting signage. And, of all things, installing a little railway! It was parallel to the wooden verandas that joined most of the real and pretend buildings along the main road.

Under normal circumstances, Poor Woolly would have been excited by the prospects of a railway through The Landing. The closest was at West Bay Road, some distance west, not that a train had been through there in years either. Today he was unfazed by what should have been cause for excitement, focused as he was on his plan for the day – or rather, on an evolving plan.

It had seemed simple enough in the early morning light of his bedroom, but in the full light of day, confronted by the physicality of it, he was filled with uncertainty.

He parked himself on the bench where he had last seen Blair, the veranda of the Owl Mountain Credit Union, the pretend credit union opposite the real post office. Even this he regarded steadily and cautiously for more than a few minutes, not wishing to be guyed. There, on the bench, he waited out the uncertainties of a Wednesday.

Sometimes circumstances overtake us, no matter how sophisticated and careful our plans. It only figures that an unsophisticated plan – hardly a plan at all, in this case – will be overtaken in unanticipated ways. When a pretty young woman with a clipboard and a harried look approached, Poor Woolly instinctively sat up straight and clutched his satchel defensively.

"Didn't you hear?" she asked pointedly. Then, as she looked down at her clipboard with a little frown added, "they called places."

"Places?" he repeated.

"Places," she repeated. "What's your name again?"

"Poor Woolly," he answered. Nodding over his shoulder toward the mountain behind the pretend credit union, he added, "my place has no phone. No calls."

"I don't see your name here. Are you new here?" She squinted a little as her eyes followed her forefinger down the sheet on her clipboard.

"First time on a Wednesday," he admitted.

"Well, you've been to costume, obviously." She eyed him up and down, making Poor Woolly rather uncomfortable. He was used to being ignored, not studied – at least, not at such close range. "I assume you're in the carriage house scene. You must get over there right away."

"Carriage h—"

"Yes. Carriage house. Go. They've called your place."

"Can't call my place. No phone." He stood. Clipboard Girl looked at him sharply, then broke into a fake smile, then a curt laugh.

"Good one," she said. Then, "seriously. Carriage house. Go."

Poor Woolly would have preferred to wait right there on the bench but, lost for words, he obeyed. In a funny way, for the first time in recent memory Poor Woolly fit right in – not that he usually stood out. Despite his queer ways, he was usually as much a part of the furniture, as they say, as anyone – even on a Wednesday.

Today, however, Poor Woolly was dressed as his grandfather would have a hundred years before. In fact, he was dressed *as* his grandfather: wool cap, rough linen shirt, tweed vest, plus-fours and wool stockings, all from his trunk. One can understand Clipboard Girl's mistake. Poor Woolly was kitted out in period costume just like the dozen or so extras milling about MacPhie's, which was all done over as it might have looked a century ago when it was indeed the Carriage House, a country inn.

Kenzie was there among the assembled extras awaiting instructions. It seemed that practically everyone in The Landing was there, and it made for quite a sight. Twenty or thirty middle-aged-to-elderly folk dressed as their grandparents standing or sitting around the village as it may have looked a hundred years past. But they were surrounded by people in modern dress wielding tools and equipment that might well have been from the future.

Kenzie approached and placed his hand on Poor Woolly's shoulder, perhaps in reassurance. "It's like a time warp Woolly, or an alien experiment. What's in the bag today?" He nodded to Poor Woolly's satchel.

Poor Woolly swung the bag a little awkwardly to his front and reached below the flap to retrieve its cargo. He wouldn't have shared something so personal with just anyone, but Kenzie was an exception. Poor Woolly carefully took out the old picture of his grandfather and the horse-and-buggy. Kenzie took it from him carefully and respectfully and viewed it arm's length.

"Whoa. Woolly. This is amazing – and kind of creepy, don't you think?"

Poor Woolly wasn't sure how to take that and looked nervously at his friend for a clue.

"What I mean is, you look just like your grandpa – I always said that – standing here just like him when that picture was taken. Come to life after a hundred years – just like it was Brigadoon. Just like this movie."

Poor Woolly wasn't catching on.

"I'll tell you more next visit. Look, they're getting ready for the next scene."

"Quiet on the set!" Clipboard Girl held a megaphone so close to her mouth it sounded to Poor Woolly like 'quite old shit,' which set him giggling.

"Quiet please!" Lights sprang to life all around them even though it was full-on morning, and Poor Woolly could see just fine.

"Places, please. Please go to your place."

The group started to spread out, each according to their instructions. Having none, Poor Woolly thought they were dispersing – he figured they were going home to their places. So, he turned and headed toward the crossroads.

"Cut!" A tall man with a ponytail stepped out from under a small canvas shelter that shielded a big camera and a little table laden with electronic gear. Clipboard Girl came running from the shadows, coming between that man and Poor Woolly.

"Sorry. Sorry," she kept repeating over her shoulder as she approached Poor Woolly. "Twenty-six. You shouldn't be here. You should be at your place."

She looked from Poor Woolly to her clipboard, to Poor Woolly again. Narrowing her eyes, she asked, "Where is your place?"

Poor Woolly turned so he could point to the west, up the mountain behind MacPhie's pretend carriage house.

"I don't think so." Clipboard Girl consulted her sheet again.

"You're not really in this scene, are you. You're not one of my extras, are you."

At this point, the man with the ponytail approached them, asking, "is everything alright? Can we get back to our places? We're losing the light."

Poor Woolly looked around at all the lights, but could not tell if any were missing or lost, or broken.

"I'm so sorry," Clipboard Girl pleaded. "This man is an extra extra – I mean, he's not on the roll. He doesn't have a place."

Poor Woolly motioned as if to provide some context when Kenzie stepped up to help. "I think Woolly got mixed up in things because of the way he's dressed today."

In unison, Clipboard Girl and Ponytail looked from Poor Woolly to Kenzie and back.

"He's dressed for a part," said Ponytail.

"Well, yes and no. The clothes belonged to Woolly's grandfather. With all the excitement and construction for your film, I think he wanted to fit in."

"Wanted to meet Blair. Blair Warner – Lisa – is in the movie. She's not a hundred. Just a pretend hundred. In a pretend village. Pretend Christmas. My grandpa's village. Not Owl Mountain. Not Kensington. MacIntosh Mountain. My place is..." Poor Woolly hesitated. With a sheepish look to Clipboard Girl, he added, "my place is MacIntosh Mountain."

Poor Woolly remembered and retrieved the photo of his grandfather. He handed it to Kenzie, who turned it so Ponytail and Clipboard Girl could see. "William. Woolly's grandpa."

"Poor Woolly," he was corrected. "William is my grandpa."

Clipboard Girl suddenly took a digital watch from among the laminated ID cards, keys and dollar-store trinkets tethered around her neck. The rattle distracted Poor Woolly, and he failed to draw her attention to the picture. Ponytail, on the other hand, did take an interest. Gently, kindly, he turned it in Kenzie's hands so that he could give it his attention without upsetting Poor Woolly.

"You're dressed just like him," Ponytail smiled.

"Just like him," Poor Woolly responded. "Just like William, my grandpa. His clothes. My memories. That's a MacPhie carriage." He cocked his head so as to share the view with Ponytail, and he pointed to the horse-and-buggy. "A real carriage, not pretend...."

"Maybe your William's clothes should be in my movie— Woolly, is it? Would you like that? Kelly here," he nodded toward Clipboard Girl, "will see that you get a contract, and we will pay you as an extra."

Clipboard Kelly's necklace of cards and watch made way for her lists as she made an exaggerated effort to comply. A look from Ponytail brought her up short and, after a split-second attitude adjustment, she tried to take charge again.

∞∞

Paperwork satisfied, Poor Woolly was seated on an antique bench on the carriage house veranda, his precious satchel on his lap and his grandpa's tweed cap crumpled nervously in his hands. To a bystander, it could have been 1909. He could have been William.

Poor Woolly felt connected with his ancestors as never before – though they would perhaps have disapproved of his motive.

The instructions were simple. "Pretend you are waiting for someone. It's okay to look around, but don't say anything, okay? And don't move from your spot, okay? And say nothing, okay?" Clipboard Kelly was patronizing him, he knew, but he let that go.

"Ready on set," someone called from somewhere. Then, "places everyone." Clipboard Kelly looked straight at Poor Woolly and gave him a look with a tiny shake of her head.

"Action." Ponytail fiddled with his headset and sat down out of sight under the little canopy. After a brief pause, a man came into view pulling a large camera mounted on the little railroad; the camera was pointed toward a man and a woman in costume who walked casually between the rails and the veranda where Poor Woolly was fairly itching with anticipation.

Behind him, there was a little commotion as a door opened and closed. He sensed a shift in people's attention and couldn't help but turn his head in response to see that his idol had made an appearance behind him.

Slack-jawed and wide-eyed, the urge to leap to his feet in defiance of his instructions nearly overpowered him. His hands instinctively moved to his sides as if to lever himself to his feet; only a 'don't-you-dare' look from Clipboard Kelly prevented it. The tension made Poor Woolly very uncomfortable, and the urge to speak – to stand – was like a powerful itch the doctor won't let you scratch. Blair Warner vs. Clipboard Kelly. Ponytail vs. Poor Woolly.

Then, as if in slow motion, Poor Woolly's non-plan started to unravel, and there was nothing he could do about it. As Kenzie later told it – and he often did – 'It was like a scene out of a movie,' a joke that gave him immense pleasure.

Mr. Trainer's Newfie dog, Bear, came roaring up the road, and up the veranda steps headed for Poor Woolly's lap, dislodging Poor Woolly's once-teen idol in the process. If Poor Woolly had kept his seat, it would have been like a dream. Instead, it was a nightmare.

Bear ran headlong toward Poor Woolly's lap which caused him to stand in a bid to eliminate that lap, a move which in turn meant that the dog's headlong rush was right at his privates, causing him to bend at the waist in both defence and reaction. (Here in the telling, Kenzie leaps to his feet, grabs his crotch, and folds at the waist in an exaggerated performance.)

In the dog's haste, it cross-checked the actor a split second before impact with Poor Woolly. Before Ponytail could yell "cut!" Poor Woolly and Lisa butted heads with disastrous effect.

"Sit!" yelled Mr. Trainer. "Shit!" yelled Clipboard Kelly. "Cut!" yelled Ponytail. "Blair!" yelled Poor Woolly. "Blood!" she yelled.

Clipboard Kelly launched into high gear, grabbing the closest thing to a cloth compress she could find and applying it to the actor's bloodied, possibly broken nose. Unfortunately for Poor Woolly, that makeshift compress was his grandfather's tweed driving cap.

"No!" he cried, instinctively reaching out to retrieve the precious artifact. The move startled Lisa. Perhaps thinking it was a further threat, she pulled back, slapping away Poor Woolly's outstretched hand – but not before he had retaken the blood-stained cap.

He was mortified, of course, and immediately took a step backward out of reach of a potential follow-up blow. Emotions he'd not felt since grade school welled up inside him, but it felt like he had no control over the outcome. He didn't want to cry, and it was not in his nature to lash out, so he just stood there, head down. Bloodied cap in a ball in his left hand, he fumbled in his satchel with his right, producing after a moment one of his grandpa's checkered handkerchiefs. This he timidly proffered to the actor with apologetic tenderness.

This time it was Clipboard Kelly who slapped away his offering. "Haven't you done enough?!" she snarled.

Kenzie, the only friendly face in the crowd that Poor Woolly could see – stepped to the fore in defence of reason. "Here now. No need for that. It was an accident."

"Accident," echoed Poor Woolly, looking from one face to another and beyond them to where all filming activity stood still. The whole village – real and pretend – seemed to hold its breath, waiting to shake it off, or to cry, or to laugh. The dog, Bear, was first to move on with her life, nuzzling first Poor Woolly, then Lisa, as if in empathy and apology respectively. Bear turned her head, leaving a healthy deposit of drool on the star's shoulder, stooped as she was yet.

The dog's movement burst the bubble surrounding the five key players in the little drama, as though someone had pressed 'play.' Without letting go of her officious appendage and papers, Clipboard Kelly held Poor Woolly's grandpa's hanky to Lisa's face – a face now very pale despite the makeup, the blood and the discoloration of a growing bruise. Clipboard Kelly kept up her attack with the handkerchief like an abstract artist attacking a blank canvas, alternately dabbing and rubbing the red blood and the dog's translucent slobber.

Poor Woolly retreated ever-so-slightly, eyeing Clipboard Kelly both fearfully and respectfully as he watched his grandfather's checkered hanky become increasingly gross. He wanted to retrieve it in the worst way. He understood its importance in the drama, but it was for him a precious heirloom at risk of being ruined, or even lost if he didn't get it back soon.

He reached for it tentatively – reaching, withdrawing, each reach a little closer. Clipboard Kelly brushed his hand aside again when, in her opinion, it got too close to her star, who she continued to swab with obsession but little effect. The actor was recovering her poise and regaining enough composure to start taking stock of the situation.

"I'm fine," she tried to brush off Clipboard Kelly's persistent assault. "I think I should go clean up."

Ponytail finally took charge and, with a nod of his head toward the pretend pharmacy, behind which could be seen a sleek white trailer, he instructed Clipboard Kelly to take Lisa to her dressing room. "Take thirty, everyone. We resume in thirty minutes if Lisa is able. We're going to lose some daylight – you all know what you have to do. Thirty minutes."

Four tattooed young men leapt to their feet and headed toward an equipment van behind the pretend tannery. Clipboard Kelly, now positively matronly, took Lisa gently by the elbow and started to lead her away.

"Wait!" Poor Woolly cried. Once again everything stopped. A rather surly look came over Clipboard Kelly as she turned toward the interruption.

"Hanky," Poor Woolly said sheepishly.

Clipboard Kelly looked down at the grossness that was once Poor Woolly's grandpa's handkerchief. "You're kidding," she pronounced.

"My grandpa's. From my trunk. That was his hanky. His hat. They came from Scotland. His father's. They came from Scotland. The hanky and the hat, and," he nodded downward at his attire, "This is Harris Tw—" he stopped suddenly and looked wide-eyed at the tweed cap in his hand, now stained almost completely by Lisa's blood.

Everyone still proximate looked as one to Poor Woolly for more reaction. Lisa spoke quietly but distinctly. "Oh look. I've spoiled your cap. Your grandpa's cap is covered with my blood. I'm so sorry..." she hesitated, wanting to use his name, but certain she hadn't paid attention and didn't know it for sure.

"Woolly," offered Kenzie.

"Poor Woolly," corrected the subject of their attention.

"He means well." Kenzie sounded apologetic, though he didn't intend to be.

To her credit, Lisa took a moment and, taking stock of the situation, took the blood-stained hanky from Clipboard Kelly and held it out to Poor Woolly.

"I'm afraid I've ruined it, Woolly, as well as the cap. I'm very sorry. Yours is a lovely costume. I'm afraid I've ruined your part in the movie, haven't I? Can you forgive me?"

Poor Woolly took the handkerchief gingerly and looked up to see her face so as to measure her sincerity. He was accustomed to reading people's true thoughts in their faces, but he was taken aback by what he saw on hers. Beneath the sincere empathy expressed through her eyes, Poor Woolly was confronted by the damage inflicted just a few moments before – though it seemed hours ago now.

He instinctively clutched the items a little more possessively. As he did, a new thought came to him, and he felt a warming sensation in a way he seldom did, one which he could never explain, a feeling which in turn warmed his face as he blushed. He may have teared up a bit too. Fortunately that was fleeting so as not to add further drama.

His heirlooms, he realized, were now precious for an entirely different reason. They – his grandfather's tweed cap and checkered hanky – were now soaked in Lisa Whelchel's blood. Blair Warner's blood. Her disfigurement would pass, but his memory of the incident, aided by the artifacts, would remain with him for good. He would forever be able to lay claim to having come face-to-face with Blair Warner – a pun lost on him but not on Kenzie, who snickers about it even now.

"Woolly," Lisa said, interrupting his reverie, "if we found you another cap to wear this once, would you still like to be in our movie?"

"Yes. Yes, I could be in your movie. My grandpa could still be in your movie. He came from Scotland. Lots of people around here came from Scotland. From Lewis. That's an island. From Lewis. From Skye. From Lochaber. They knew about fishing. They didn't know how to farm. They knew about cattle. They knew a lot about horses...." Poor Woolly's voice drifted off under a look of impatience from Clipboard Kelly. "Joe MacInnis has horses," he finished weakly.

The right moment had arrived for Clipboard Kelly to ease her star out of and away from the conversation and toward her trailer, from which they emerged after about half an hour, Lisa's face freshly painted.

"Places! Everyone. To your places please." Donning his headset, Ponytail once again took his seat behind the cameras. "Places. Quiet please."

Poor Woolly hesitated for a split second, his place in the movie was on the bench on the veranda. Whether or not Lisa sensed his hesitation, she slipped her hand under Poor Woolly's elbow and walked gently with him to the bench. "We're doing it a little differently this time Woolly. They're not doing a close-up, so we can just sit here and have a nice little chat."

"What do we talk about?"

"Action!" yelled Ponytail from his hidden seat.

"Well, you already know something about me. Tell me more about you. Your people came from Scotland. Mine came from Texas. I guess you have lived here all of your life?"

"My life so far. My mother's and my father's parents came from Scotland, from Lewis. That's an island. I've never been there. I went to a city once. Not in Scotland. In Canada. My sis—"

"So your grandfather was from Lewis, and these are his clothes." She took the lapel of his jacket gently between her thumb and fingers.

"His father's clothes. I have his trunk in my pl—" He hesitated, then clarified, "in my house."

And so it went for ten or fifteen or maybe more minutes, all the while people, actors and crew, and cameras and lights moved around them as in some magical dance. Poor Woolly was almost oblivious to all that, lost as he was in the glow of Blair Warner's undivided attention.

∞∞

"Lisa! My friend Lisa Whelchel!" Finally!

Poor Woolly had missed most of December. He even missed two Tuesdays; Kenzie twice had to deliver his groceries. Like everyone, but more than anyone, Poor Woolly was glued to his TV, watching every Hallmark Christmas movie programmed that month. Twenty-five of them. An Advent calendar of red wool coats with fake fur collars, of bright eyes and rosy cheeks. For Poor Woolly it was an Advent calendar with only one treat, but he had to watch them all to get it.

Many of the movies looked the same, and they told almost the same story in almost the same pretend towns, with, he now knew, pretend names. Kenzie had shown him how to pause the picture, and he read the closing credits carefully. He counted six in Banff, five in Aspen, four in Bethel, Maine, three in Harpers Ferry, three in Almonte, Ontario, and of course the three in The Landing. There was one in New York City too.

∞∞

Still flushed and flustered by her brush with fame, Bossy was holding court in the post office on the first Tuesday after Christmas, when Poor Woolly went in to check his mail.

"Here's Woolly. We are very proud of you, Woolley. Did you see me in the movie?" Mayor Bossy asked.

Poor Woolly smiled shyly, took his candy and quietly retreated. It was Tuesday, but he supposed Bossy and others went to the Post office almost every day.

fin

A WING AND A PRAYER

John Norman MacDonald is a human equivalent of a double-edged sword – at once the most praised and the most cursed man in two counties.

He is heavy of foot but light of touch. He has the biggest gut but the littlest mutt, the biggest truck but the littlest house. He has a foul tongue but a big heart. He's a redneck and an artist. He works every day, plays every night, yet never gets off his arse.

You might expect such a large fellow to be known as "Tiny," for nicknames are often ironic. But John Norman MacDonald is either known as that – John Norman MacDonald – or as Tim. And not because of his size – you know, as in Tiny Tim. And not just because of the month of emptied Tim Hortons cups on the dash of his backhoe.

Nicknames are sometimes of complicated construction in Cape Breton. There are actual studies on the subject! It's Tim because he carries with him a donut seat cushion wherever he goes. Get it? Donut = Tim Hortons = Tim.

John Norman, Tim, is a gifted heavy equipment operator who has an artistic side. A snow plow driver in winter, a backhoe operator in summer, a backyard mechanic in evenings and a piano accompanist on weekends. Thus, he has spent practically his whole life on his arse – it's a wonder the man can stand – and the donut seat cushion protects what's left of it from torn seats, piano benches and church pews, not that Tim has spent much time in church. Being an entrepreneur and all, he never took much stock in church – he gets through life by the seat of his pants, so to speak.

Not the engineer he might have been, not the fiddler he could have been, from jackhammer to felt hammer, Tim's delicate touch at the controls and at the keyboard is a wonder to behold. He can thread-the-needle with a backhoe on a Saturday morning, and "strip-the-willow" at Glencoe on a Saturday night.

Got a hole to fill in? Call Tim. Need a percussionist to fill in? Call Tim. And you can count on Tim because he doesn't drink.

Tim can play a tune on anything. He feels the rhythm. But for a period of about four months every year, that's a problem. It's not a problem when he's play-ing, it's a problem when he's plowing.

Like I said, Tim can find the rhythm and play the tune – including behind the wheel. Chugging forty klicks up Cenotaph Road, he's humming "Neil Gow's Lament"; at sixty going down he's whistling "The Blackthorn Strathspey"

At eighty, he's leaving the village to "Sleepy Maggie." Tim gets that snow plow slinging along, the slush and snow fairly dancing off fence posts, mailboxes, highway signs and guardrails in syncopation, punctuated here and there by the sickly 'ping' of gravel on a decrepit phone-service access box, or the 'double-clunk' of an accidentally decapitated mailbox.

With the wing down, Tim can Highland fling the snow and ice clear to the treetops, from where it returns to earth as thunderous applause. If the wind is right, you can hear Tim's playful plowing clear across the loch, depending on which side of the road he's on. It's a beauty to behold.

Some road noise can be irritating in the quiet of the library, the church or the school, and downright annoying when you are trying to have a serious but quiet conversation in the Carriage Makers Café. But this is Cape Breton. People here tap their feet in time with church music and Christmas carols, so a proper sense of rhythm is respected. Here, the whine of snow tires is a tenor drone and the chains are sleigh bells.

Being a snowplow operator is an honourable profession, one with the right balance of power and service. A lesser being would have earned more than one black eye or broken nose in retaliation for missing mailboxes and highway signs, but John Norman MacDonald is the best damn accompanist in two counties. Not to be blasphemous or anything, Tim was God-like in his command of the keyboard Sunday afternoons in Judique.

And let's be serious. Who is going to say something negative to a burly backhoe operator who, if he so desired, could do serious damage to property or person. Roadside destruction is simply part of winter life in rural Cape Breton. Not that there is an urban Cape Breton. Snow life includes a delicate dance between shovellers, snow blowers and snow plowers – a goodnatured test of stamina. Usually.

But sometimes a man snaps – even a good man like now-retired Father Red Beaton, formerly from Creignish. Time was, a priest could retire in the glebe house while a younger man moved in and took over the parish. Nowadays, however, with the Church selling off real estate in atonement, retired priests are just like us – struggling to afford a little Cape Cod house for themselves and, sometimes, their long-time housekeepers.

So it was for Fr. Red Beaton. But, accustomed to having things done for him by parishioners seeking indulgences, Fr. Red, was having difficulty adjusting his expectations to new surroundings. He was used to a modicum of deference, and everyone's lack of respect for the speed limit around his newly acquired resting place was – well, let's just say that Tim's God-like command of the winter roads was less than holy in the eyes of Fr. Red. He regarded all music and dancing with some suspicion; to him, Tim's snow plow symphony was the heavy equipment equivalent of devil's music.

With neither a sense of rhythm, nor sense of humour, and after umpteen years in the pulpit in the thankless pursuit of balancing good and evil, Fr. Red was in retirement wholly lacking in charity. His first winter on this side of the island was a fairly easy one – more rain than snow, and less wind meant less drifting. Fr. Red's meticulous manual clearing worked just fine and, despite their clucking of tongues and shaking of heads, he ignored local advice that he should invest in a gas-powered snow blower.

True to form, the next winter's weather was positively biblical. Fr. Red thought that hell had indeed frozen over, and he along with it. But he feared little less than God and the bishop, much less the weather and, as his housekeeper watched over him from the front window, he often defied the elements to clear the demon snow during the height of a storm.

Tim, of course, was in his element in such conditions, and by January he was already halfway to plowing through a new tune. Tone deaf Fr. Red couldn't get the hang of the tune or the timing. It's a good thing that lightning storms are a rarity in winter, for Fr. Red might have been struck dead through his upraised snow shovel as he gestured in Tim's rear-views in a manner unbecoming a man of the cloth.

It's not that Tim is the unholy sort or is mean-spirited. He just does his job with a flourish. The priest might have respected that, for he was known for his own flourishes from the pulpit. But he went over to the dark side that winter. If he couldn't count on Tim seeing the light on his own, Fr. Red would teach him.

On the advice of his neighbours – good people who understand how things work around here – he knew he couldn't call on Tim's bosses to change Tim's tune. As opposed to waiting for a sign from above, Fr. Red created a sign of his own, one that Tim and other speeders could understand.

On a mild day between snow storms – one of those days when the consistency of the snow changes from sandy to sticky – and with the help of his housekeeper, Fr. Red built a substantial snowman, right beside the road at the end of the long row of tall, perfectly spaced pine trees to the left of the house. Tim's plow always thrummed those pines perfectly.

They dressed the snowman in one of Fr. Red's old cassocks, and topped it with a wide-brimmed felt hat. An oversized placard on a long stake shouted a glaring message for all speeders, cars and plows alike:

SLOW DOWN
FOR CHRIST'S SAKE!

∞∞

Fr. Red had failed to take into account two fateful factors: Tim's dedication to his job and falling temperatures. It had not snowed for a few days, so it came as a bit of a surprise when the unmistakable beat of Tim's approaching snow plow-cum-drum-machine penetrated Fr. Red's living room where he was settled in for a quiet evening of television.

Tim was out pushing back the snow banks to make way for a forecasted nor'easter. The extra shift was a blessing, for winter was rapidly coming to an end and he really wanted to finish a new set of tunes he'd been working on. Lost in his musical reverie, he accelerated toward Fr. Red's towering perfectly-spaced pine trees anticipating that his truck's massive wing plow would surely thump out the transition from slow air to Strathspey, like the quickening feet of an experienced audience.

Suddenly, out of the darkness and into the headlights sprang Fr. Red's cloaked snow-priest and its glaring invective.

"Cheezuss!"

Tim instinctively yanked hard on the wheel to miss the figure, bringing the tip of the wing in exaggerated acceleration to catch the snow-priest square in the midriff. Believe it or not, the mass of the now-frozen-solid structure actually caused the entire truck to snap around like a guard dog at the end of a chain. Despite Tim's expertise, his truck headed straight up Fr. Red's driveway, charging at the fear-frozen figure of the old priest, snow shovel raised in self-defence.

Having heard the plow in the distance, and wanting to clean up whatever bit of snow would be left behind, Fr. Red had donned the full-length black overcoat hanging beside his back door, pulled on his black, wide-brimmed hat, and stepped out onto the stoop, grabbing his snow shovel as he passed.

On reaching the driveway, he was confronted by two gigantic fireballs from hell bearing down on him with an un-Godly roar, the truck's glaring headlights high atop the grinning steel plow sparking off his expensive asphalt.

Inside the cab of the truck, Tim had yet to regain his composure when he spotted the priest in his headlights, shovel upraised, like the one he had already struck. There was, he understandably thought, a posse of priests come to life to haunt him into atonement.

To make matters worse, in the glow of the living room window dead ahead the silhouette of the housekeeper throwing back the curtains to see what was going on, in that instant appeared to Tim as a conjurer invoking an incantation.

Tim jumped on the brake pedal with both feet for maximum effect, which lifted his arse clear off his seat, freeing his special cushion, which – following the laws of inertia – promptly left the seat and landed at his feet.

Almost stopped, Tim slammed the truck into reverse. But without the cushion, he sat a full six inches lower in the seat, making his rear-views of little use and, wing still extended, the plow backhanded what was left of the snow priest on the way out for good measure. Tim held on for dear life as the truck – still in reverse – hightailed it blindly up Cenotaph Road, back-up beeper keeping time with his pounding heart.

∞∞

It was a blessing for both Fr. Red and John Norman that there were no storms requiring snow removal for a couple of weeks. They'd no desire to come into contact with one another and risk reliving their respective traumas.

Fr. Red did knuckle under and purchase a gas-powered snow blower when they went on sale that spring, and Tim did finish his tune. When he and the boys played it in a set for the first time in public a few Saturdays ago, he was really pleased with the response. The set starts with "Cenotaph Air," followed by "The Pine Trees Strathspey" and, finally, "The Reverse Reel."

"That's a new set," smiled one of the breathless dancers afterward, "what d'ya call it?"

"A Wing and a Prayer, Buddy," Tim reflected from atop his favourite cushion, "A Wing and a Prayer."

fin

SANDY NEAL'S LAST RIDE

"**S**hotgun!"

Surely every male growing up in North America has shouted that clarion call at least once in their lifetime – and pretty safe odds that they've shouted it more than once. If by some bizarre twist of fate or isolation they haven't said it, they have heard it.

"Shotgun!" complete with capital 'S' and exclamation, was reportedly Sandy Neal MacDonald's first word. Not "Ma," or "Da," not "bubba" or "boobie," or "zinc oxide" – "Shotgun!"

Phonsie Sampson once said that Sandy Neal loved anything on wheels. "If it's moving, 'e is into it,"

When Sandy Neal turned ninety, which was a few months after they took away his driver's licence, he ran away from the home. He left in the middle of the night, hot-wired a neighbour's lawn tractor and hightailed it up and over MacIntosh Mountain. They cornered him – naked as the day he was born – racing down Big Brook Road toward the 105. That must have been a sight. I guess it's true what Phonsie says: we start life as children and if we live long enough – or too long – we get child-like again before we leave. "Stunned as a partridge, naked as a jay-bird."

Given his age, I imagined Sandy Neal's first "Shotgun!" was on a buckboard behind actual horse power, as opposed to engine horsepower. The Landing was a far cry from the wild-wild west, but the roads around the West Bay of Loch Bras d'Or were in fact pretty wild in the 1920s and 30s. Running the horses into town for supplies could also mean running into a bear or a bobcat or the like. Maybe someone riding shotgun was not just some nostalgic notion.

There used to be a photograph in the office of MacPhie's Carriage Makers of a wee Sandy Neal sitting beside his uncle Calum in a brand new MacPhie's Deluxe. The look of anticipation on the boy's face is priceless. I do wish we could get our hands on that picture now.

In his working life, Sandy Neal operated a livery service, serving the communities and farmsteads between Point Tupper and Orangedale – MacDonald's Livery, it was called. He started it at an early age, probably as soon as his folks were sure a horse would listen to him. Phonsie said he was "at 'ome 'ome on de reins."

Sandy Neal quickly earned a reputation for his complete horsemanship, complete because he never mistreated the animals in his care, never pushed them harder or faster than he knew they were capable of, and because those horses and his gear were always spotless and in good working order.

Don't get me wrong, Sandy Neal was no Sunday surrey driver. He liked to go fast if the horses were willing, just not so fast as to risk injury to them or to him – usually.

Hector Doink MacDonald, no relation, from over Inverness, once told the story of a trip he took with Sandy Neal from Orangedale to Point Tupper. Hector Doink had missed the train at the former, and needed to catch up before it was loaded onto the ferry at the latter. Sandy Neal had a hitch of four on because he had just delivered a second-hand boat motor from Malagawatch to a fisherman in MacKinnon's Harbour.

"We fairly flew," remembered Hector Doink. "He took every turn at the same speed. There was this one turn we met a car coming the other way. I thought we were done for, but Sandy Neal rounded that corner on two wheels and two horses; I swear, the hooves of the two airborne horses knocked the cap off the Yankee who was driving that car – and probably two years off his life.

"Once we were past, Sandy Neal just set the team and the rig back on all corners like he done it every day – and maybe he did." Hector Doink was a great one for the stories.

∞∞

There were only a few cars and trucks owned by people in the early days. Some of the merchants had them, but not many others. This was partly out of respect for the carriage maker in the village; finding a balance between the means of the old ways and the needs of the new wasn't always easy.

MacPhie carriages relied on people needing them, and the tanneries – and the sawmill – relied on the carriage maker making them, etc. You can see the problem for those whose businesses or jobs were made better by the increase in productivity made possible by a pickup truck, for example. Cars and trucks that were made in God-knows-where seemed more efficient than horses – and not as smelly. People gravitated toward them for a number of reasons – some good, some not so.

Over time, cars and trucks simultaneously became symbols of prosperity and symbols of impoverishment

– the demise of businesses and services consequently abandoned their wood-shingled premises.

But Sandy Neal's love of driving saw him through. He loved his horse power *and* saw the business sense of horsepower. Another carriage customer down the drain.

Some men might have sold the horses for meat, but Sandy Neal put them out to pasture, where they became part of the scenery – loved by passing tourists, lamented by aging locals. He was quick to make the change "from leather switch to starter switch," Phonsie said, "from delivery to DE-livery." Sandy Neal's sense of balance, timing and some would say, an understanding of physics assured his easy transition.

That the transition was both practical and pleasurable made it all the more swift, and people up and down the loch quickly became used to the sight of the still-youngish Sandy Neal in his dark green Ford stake-box truck leading a cloud of dust. The driver's side window was always wide open, his sinewy horse-trained forearm hanging out, and his head cocked at just the right angle to catch the sun and the wind without catching a rock in the face.

If you think the mass and power of the truck slowed him down some, "you've got another think coming," as Phonsie would say. Similar to his care for the horses, Sandy Neal kept his cars and trucks spotless and running smoothly.

My mental picture of Sandy Neal changed little over the years. Yes, approaching middle age, his window was up more often so he could hear the radio, or his wife – sometimes both – but his hands grasped the wheel as lightly as they had the reins. His foot stayed firmly planted on the accelerator. Phonsie joked that Sandy Neal's wife had one leg longer than the other from slamming on a phantom brake pedal at every bend in the road.

Sandy Neal and his missus didn't have any children that survived. When business was slow, or just for the pleasure of it, he used to take us village kids for long rides down to Marble Mountain or over to St. Peter's – anywhere the wind took us, really. We'd have our heads and arms out the window, just like Sandy Neal. Out of the corner of my eye, when it was my turn to ride shotgun, I could see him, one hand on the wheel, elbow out the window and craning his neck to feel the wind on his face.

I'm not saying Sandy Neal invented that classic pose, but he personified it. And he was classy, not flashy or showy. He never squealed his tires like some of the young fellows did, and do, and he never made a fuss when he got a new truck. Calm and confident, that was Sandy Neal.

∞∞

We grew up. Some of us. Some moved away, some stayed around – most had their own cars, but some still had to ride shotgun. You could tell who drove and who didn't by which arm was more tanned.

It followed that since most families had their own cars, they didn't need a livery service anymore, and reluctantly Sandy Neal retired. He retired his fleet too. And just like his horses, he provided a nice home for them, tending to them on a daily basis and regularly taking one or another out for a run to keep them, and himself, in running order.

Where most men around here would retire to their shed, whittling whistles out of kindling and sharpening their tools 'til they'd cut concrete, Sandy Neal couldn't sit still. With fewer and fewer nephews and nieces to take driving, and his wife increasingly content to spend her time at her loom, Sandy Neal got a dog – a Sheltie – and named it Shotgun. The dog rode in style, sitting bolt upright in Sandy Neal's pickup, head and paw out the window, tongue and ears lapping the wind.

∞∞

Time, as they say, waits for no man, nor his dog. Funny thing about time – the older one gets, the faster time seems to pass. Yet the older one gets, the slower one drives. Phonsie says it's like we go from 'Sunday drivers' to 'someday drivers.' That was the case even with Sandy Neal. He and the dog cruised up and down the road at a pace that ensured they didn't miss anything and that used up the maximum allowable time for an outing.

Shotgun reached an acceptable age in dog-years, but met an untimely end when, in a momentary lapse of some sort, Sandy Neal lost control of his old Mercury Crown Vic' on County Line Road and slammed into a tree. Blessedly, the dog died instantly. Sandy Neal's injuries were only to his pride, though that pain was deep and prolonged.

He'd been driving cars for more than seventy years, horses before that, all without sustaining anything worse than a chipped windshield and a chipped tooth. In the eyes of the authorities, on the other hand, he'd been driving for more than seventy years, and that was long enough so far as they were concerned. They took away his licence.

To his way of thinking, Sandy Neal didn't have a licence when he moved from shotgun to the reins to the stick shift, and damned if he was going to move back. He'd spent his whole life in control – to suddenly be a passenger was just too much. He got caught behind the wheel a couple of times, thanks to tips from safety-minded but humourless neighbours. Sandy Neal's wife passed away; what was left of his family decided he was a danger to himself and insisted he go into the old folks' home.

He resisted, of course. Sitting around watching old Steve MacQueen movies was far too sedentary a lifestyle for Sandy Neal – "sedimentary," Phonsie phrased it: "sittin' 'round like ol' rocks." That's when he took the joy ride I was telling you about. Of course, the fact that he showed them a whole lot more than his moxie, being naked and all, pretty much sealed his fate.

It wasn't too long after that his ride was over. I wish I could tell you that he met his maker in an act of vehicular defiance, like Steve MacQueen, or *Thelma and Louise*. The truth is, he just gave up.

∞∞

Me and Phonsie were among those who road shotgun while Sandy Neal was waked. By that I mean we sat up with the body in his old house next to the livery, both now owned by his cousin's son, Calum Beag. It was Phonsie who said it was like we were riding shotgun for the old fellow on his last ride. "The old boy'd roll over in 'is grave if 'e knew about all dis fuss," he said aloud more than once.

I mentioned in an offhand sort of way that it would have been more fitting to wake him in the livery barn next door. It was still standing, more or less, and still housed a couple of old cars and Sandy Neal's last Ford pickup. Calum Beag told me he was holding out to get higher prices for them. Can't blame a fellow for that.

Well, when I mentioned the wake and the livery, a strange look came over Phonsie, like his eyes would pop out of his head. They might have too, if his grin wasn't so wide that his rum-rosy cheeks were holding them in.

It was late, and it was just me and Phonsie and a couple of the boys, Seamus and Angus, left to take care of things. According to custom, we all had a bit of a glow on – the kind of glow that is easily sparked to full-blown devilment. Phonsie stood, emptied his glass, set it down firmly among the sweets on a little table; hitched up his trousers, and declared, "Come on b'ys. Time fer Sandy Neal's las' ride."

It took only one try to learn that we wouldn't be able to lift casket and body as a single unit, the preferred option for me – one that avoided having to manhandle the old fellow. I didn't know for sure of any curses associated with touching a dead body, and I didn't want to learn of any either. I hoped the others felt the same. It should have been easy to lay the coffin in the bed of the pickup truck for what I expected would be a quick ride through the village before returning him unmolested to his waking place.

Undeterred, Phonsie motioned me to join him at the feet, and Seamus and Angus to the head and shoulders. After a few grunts, a few curses and some inebriated giggling, we managed to get the old man out of the coffin and to his feet. Phonsie got behind him. By wrapping his arms almost around Sandy Neal he was able to get him to take a few Frankenstein steps toward the kitchen and thence out the side door of the house.

Built like the Acadian fisherman he is, Phonsie is a human coconut: medium height and a hairy barrel of a chest that served to shorten his bulging arms. Despite Sandy Neal's slight frame, frailed by age and death, Phonsie couldn't quite link his hands in front to secure his bear hug, and I was concerned that he would lose hold of the old fellow.

"'Ere. Piggy-back 'im," Phonsie told Seamus, who was hanging on to the porch railing like he was on the pitching deck of a rudderless boat. But Seamus was always game and rarely argued with Phonsie. They were cousins and deck mates on Phonsie's old man's lobster boat. Seamus let go of the railing and moved in front of Sandy Neal, turned around and, hands on his knees to help him take the weight, backed into the old man who was now leaning forward from the waist.

I had no doubt that Seamus could manage such a load sober, but had serious doubts under the present circumstances. Sure enough, when Phonsie let go, Sandy Neal pitched stiffly forward and downward. Without so much as an instant of hesitation in which he could take evasive action, Seamus was flattened to the ground.

You should have heard him howl! Seamus that is. I think he was yelling "Jesus, get him off me! Get him off me!" That's what I'd be yelling. But his cries were muffled like he'd been buried alive and squirming like Sandy Neal was in there with him – which of course he was.

The more Seamus squirmed and tried to get out from under the body, the more animated the body became on top. Anyone witnessing the porch-lit scene from a distance would think the two were wrestling, with Sandy Neal having the upper hand. An audience of three – me and Phonsie and Angus – sat cheering from the porch steps. We were sitting because we were helpless with laughter and consequently incapable of being any help.

Our convulsions must have had a bit of a sobering effect because after a few moments, it occurred to me that we were likely making too much noise and risking discovery.

"Cheesuss! What's the penalty for messing with a dead body?" I asked. That stopped Phonsie mid-laugh, and we both looked and listened for signs of life in the nearer houses, though they were probably a safe distance from our efforts. We had Calum Beag's house to ourselves for waking Sandy Neal. The livery was among the ghostly remains of the former carriage works and the former tanneries, and across the road from the village green and the old wharf that gave The Landing its name. The nearest house was Dr. MacKay's, and the family that lived there slept on the water side of it.

Phonsie and I moved to disengage Sandy Neal from Seamus, who was not laughing as he leapt to his feet and frantically dusted off the front of his clothes. "I gotta go home and shower," he said, and hurriedly headed up the road as Phonsie and I, with Angus coaching, worked on reanimating Sandy Neal – me wanting to work our way back into the house to lay him to rest again, and Phonsie wanting to continue with the plan by moving toward the livery.

"C'mon b'y. Once trou' de village for old time' sake. We can do it." Phonsie positioned himself behind the old man once more and was trying to get his feet moving again.

I was no match for the combined mass of the two of them and had to get back on board. I must say, Phonsie did a real good job of it once he got into a rhythm. The man-door in the large wooden double barn doors was never locked, we knew, and thankfully well oiled, for it opened smoothly and quietly.

Sandy Neal's old forest-green Ford stake-box pickup was closest to the doors, so while I pushed those wide, Phonsie and Angus loaded the old man into the shotgun side of the bench seat. They set his arm and head in what almost passed for the classic pose, then clambered in through the driver-side door to squeeze into the middle. I was thankful that it wasn't a more modern truck with a four-door crew cab and extra seating. I think Phonsie would have tried to sit Sandy Neal behind the wheel and to control his movements from the back seat. Anyway, barn doors open, I climbed into the driver's seat, and we crept out into the darkness in the manner of thieves.

If you know The Landing you know the village consists of only two roads – one road through it and one off that. There's no going around the block, and not what a reasonable person could call a loop. If you're not going to Marble Mountain, or to West Bay Road, or to Port Hawkesbury, then you're committed to driving a few hundred metres in one direction, turning around, and driving the few hundred metres back again. If it's the middle of the night and you've had a few and need to take a piss, The Landing is a very small place indeed.

Under the circumstances, Sandy Neal's last ride was rather anticlimactic, far less exciting in execution than in inspiration. I shut off the truck's motor, and we coasted silently down the hill, into the yard and up to the porch. While Phonsie and Angus manoeuvred the body up the two steps and through the back door to its proper place, I drove the truck back to the livery, closed things up and returned to the house, content that Sandy Neal's last ride had been the right thing to do.

Phonsie and Angus were waiting for me, towering over the body on the floor beside the waiting coffin. I'd forgotten that there were now just three of us to get the old man back into his box. There had been four to get him out with gravity on our side – now we were only three working against gravity and against time. I encouraged Angus to take charge. He was an engineer at the mill, so I figured he'd have some advantage over us in the brains department. But just because engineers are smart doesn't mean they are fast, and that left an opening for Phonsie to have another flash of brilliance.

"You boys lif' de coffin, I'll take away de saw 'orses, and you set 'er down on the floor," he instructed, which we did and he did.

"Now, turn it onto de side." Which we did. Then, catching on to the plan, Angus still at the head and me at the foot, we opened both sections of the lid and shuttled the coffin until it touched Sandy Neal. Holding the lids open with one hand, we bent over, and while Phonsie pushed at the middle we pulled at the ends and rolled the body into its white satin cocoon. The motion and additional weight helped to tip the coffin right side up, and the lids closed in unison with one satisfying thud.

First at one end, then at the other, the three of us lifted the coffin atop the saw horses without too much difficulty, and we collapsed into our seats to await dawn and the next shift of watchers.

∞∞

I awoke – still seated upright and head tilted to the back of the comfy wingback armchair I'd claimed a few hours before – to the sound and smell of coffee being made in the kitchen. Phonsie was stretched out on the settee; Angus was nowhere to be seen. Seamus hadn't returned so far as I knew. I got to my feet to stretch myself alive, tried to make myself presentable for whomever was taking over our duties and headed upstairs to use the bathroom.

Angus was coming down from there at the same time and I waited for him – bad luck to pass on the stairs – returning his boyish grin and wink as he passed. Behind me, he greeted two women from the church who, by the sounds emanating from the kitchen, were busily tidying things from the night before.

The flushing toilet and running water in the sink must have drowned out the racket in the parlour below, for when I returned, Phonsie and Angus were helping Maggie Leonard up from the floor while Mary Mhor MacDonald – no relation – righted an overturned chair. Both women were pale as paper, in stark contrast with Phonsie and Angus who were both flushed red from excitement, whatever it was. Angus caught my eye and nodded, directing my attention to the now-open coffin and the cause of the commotion.

Sandy Neal's body was lying face down in the coffin, his wrinkled shirt untucked from his trousers. The untreated bald spot on the back of his head was a deathly green.

"Told ya de ole fella'd roll over wit' all de fuss," Phonsie said matter-of-factly as he gently set Mrs. Leonard in the wingback chair.

"Well, I gotta go," Angus announced hurriedly, and as he headed for the door added, "anyone need a lift?"

"Yup," I said following him quickly.

Phonsie, close behind, called, "Shotgun!"

fin

WINTY VERSUS THE ANTS

Ants.

Winston Currie – Winty, to his friends – and Jake MacEwen, the local insurance adjuster, were standing next to each other and surveying the scene of the accident.

Ants.

Jake half-expected Winty to clap him on the back, burst into laughter and give a more plausible explanation for the gigantic white pine tree lodged in Winty's wife's second-story bedroom window.

That it was no accident was obvious. It had, quite clearly, been sawn off.

Ants. Winty made it sound like this sort of thing happened all the time.

Human errors in yard maintenance were common occurrences in Jake's line of work. He dutifully made a few notes in his logbook – the estimated size of the tree, angle of the fall, how it had crashed onto and into the house, and the obvious damage.

Winty told Jake that his wife had insisted he solve their ant problem. The tree must have been dead inside and full of ants, he told Jake – who dutifully noted that in his logbook.

As they stood there, a squirrel started making an awful racket from the upper branches of the downed tree, chirping and chattering something fierce. Winty's face went so red Jake thought he might catch fire.

Winty's wife's pale round face appeared through the smashed window, and started warding off the squirrel with a worn corn broom, which served only to excite it further. "Winston," she yelled. "Don't just stand there, do something!"

To spare Winty further embarrassment at the harassment he was getting from his wife and the squirrel, Jake distracted himself by looking around the property.

On the other side of the house, he could see the back half of Winty's shed and workshop. The shed still looked like new – and so it should. The insurance company had paid for it to be refurbished after a fire all but destroyed two sides of it two years ago.

Again, Winty's wife hollered at him to do something about the squirrel that was tormenting them all from its perch just out of her reach. Winty strode off purposefully in the direction of the shed, leaving Jake to his thoughts.

Jake recalled that the shed fire had not spread beyond two walls, but the claim had been substantial, considering the size of the building.

It had been terrorized by a squirrel, including chewing partially through the wiring – wiring unquestionably installed by do-it-yourself Winty. Though not schooled in any particular trade, like a lot of men around here Winty was pretty handy around his various projects.

He'd wanted to leave out poisoned bait for the squirrel, but his wife forbade it for fear her cat would get into it, which would have been fine with Winty. Instead, he had baited one of those spring-loaded rat traps with pine nuts.

The trap got tripped alright, making a satisfying snap! heard all the way to the woodpile where Winty was labouring at that moment. His self-satisfied smirk was short-lived, however – almost immediately, the squirrel started mocking him from a nearby tree.

The trap must have been tripped by something small, a mouse maybe, because it appeared that the trap had flipped upside down. The metal wire that was to end life for the squirrel sprang to life itself, shorting out the partially exposed electric wiring. That spark in turn ignited a small fire that in turn ignited an accumulation of oily rags and sawdust. To say Winty was handy, is not to say he was tidy.

Lucky for him, he was able to extinguish the fire before it reached his oil-and-paint-stained workbench and the jerry cans of fuel below it. Lucky for him. Unlucky for the insurance. The claim showed that he was not in time to prevent the substantial loss of a wall of really expensive power tools. Damaged beyond salvage, it was reported, they had to be replaced.

He'd had them for years, Winty had sworn. No receipts.

∞∞

Back to the matter at hand. Jake thought his skepticism might be showing when he saw Winty coming purposefully toward him with a shotgun over his arm.

"Just to scare 'er," he told Jake. "It's not loaded. Can't shoot near the house anyway. Neighbours might get nosy." His intended target was now nowhere to be seen, or heard.

"You'll get her one day, Winston." Using the client's proper name kept things on a more professional level.

∞∞

The extensive and expensive collection of shiny new tools purchased after the fire was not the only reminder of Winty's long battle with the squirrel. There was also his wife's a big-screen TV, the corner of which could be seen through the damaged bedroom window.

As Jake recalled it, last year had been particularly dry almost into October. As we all know, when the evenings start to cool in September, small creatures start preparing for winter by finding and claiming a cozy spot to build and provision their nests.

With the shed no longer safe, the squirrel had apparently sought and found a perfect spot elsewhere on the property – a drainage pipe that normally discharged into the ditch down at the road. It was nice and dry – like I said, it was a very dry year.

Winty had witnessed the squirrel's numerous trips with nesting materials and decided to put a stop to it by flushing it out. He shoved a garden hose into the drainage pipe through an access port he'd made for just such a purpose. Unfortunately, just as he turned on the water his wife called him away to one chore or another, and he forgot about his plan. The hose ran for a couple of hours, but the squirrel had blocked things up solid, and all Winty accomplished was filling the pipe.

Remember that once-in-a-hundred-years storm in early October last year? Well, the drainage system around the house was already full, thanks to the squirrel, and all that rain had nowhere to go except to backup into the basement of the house.

According to Jake's report, the flood damage included a big screen TV and an exercise treadmill Winty had apparently stored down there while he did some renovations. They weren't new, so he didn't have receipts, and the insurance covered their replacement costs, along with extensive renovations to the basement. A brand new big screen TV now hung in his wife's bedroom, and a new state-of-the-art treadmill was gathering dust in Winty's half-finished basement man cave.

∞∞

Jake gave his head a shake back to the present, alerted by a squirrel – perhaps *the* squirrel – chattering once again from the upper branches of the downed pine tree still lodged in the side of the house. Through the smashed bedroom window, a muffled but undeniably wife-like voice hollered "Winston!"

The squirrel chimed in too, whether mocking Winty or warning him we'll never know.

"You've had a run of bad luck here Winston, but this one takes the cake," Jake said very seriously. To himself, he thought 'this one takes the prize. A fire. A flood. Now pests. Positively biblical.'

Winty paused and cautiously nodded in the affirmative.

From above, they again heard, "Winston!"

"Are we done here Jake?" Winty asked. It was clouding over, and his wife had said there were thunderstorms brewing.

He had to get a move on to get the tree down and something over the hole before the rain got in, or the squirrel got in.

Jake agreed. He told Winty that it wouldn't do to have a wet tree in the wife's bedroom in a thunderstorm. The kind of luck Winty was having, the wet tree might get hit by lighting.

Winty looked up at the tree again. And at the window. She was just sitting up there. Daring him.

fin

A MAN OF EXCEPTIONALLY
KEEN DISCERNMENT

It's a little bit out of the way, but once in a while some celebrity or big-wig does pass through The Landing. Not that many folks could list them for you. No one pays much attention to visitors unless they make a big splash. And when that happens, people would just as soon forget.

But like I said, some do visit; the surrounding area is among the most beautiful on the whole of Cape Breton. It's something special, but we don't want anyone to think they're someone special, or even to know that someone thinks they are special. We let them be.

One celebrity who did get everyone talking for a while came to visit Kenneth McIntosh. Kenny was the surveyor – though he was really more of a scientist. He even wrote a few books, though I don't suppose anyone around here has read even one of them. His first book was named *Subsidence of the Coast of Nova Scotia*. Subsidence is when the earth settles into an abandoned mine or an old well or the like – though different than a sinkhole.

According to some, the whole country is sinking – and not just because of the Liberals. But Kenny did the math and wrote that Nova Scotia, at least, is not sinking, though I don't think he acknowledged that the ocean is rising, a distinction not lost on his detractors.

Another book was way out there, you might say, *The Evolution of Planetary Motion*. I've heard it said that he even had an idea how to create a perpetual motion machine. I'm not sure what that is, but it was something that got people pretty excited for awhile.

Anyway, most people around here are of Highland descent, so Kenny knew not to claim to be someone special – on the other hand, you can be sure that no one allowed him to, even if he was. Some say he was curious about everything, what with being university educated and smart. Others say he was just plain nosy.

∞∞

Kenny had a theory about the fireballs people saw in the sky hereabouts.

Old Mrs. Ross over on the road to Dundee told everyone that she seen a double fireball in the night sky over the loch. It shot across the heavens like out of a gun, she said, then split into two – one flew over the West Bay highlands, one along the North Mountain. She was the only one to see that one; if it wasn't for the fact that others have seen fireballs before, people would have said she was too long tending her old man's whisky still in the apple orchard up behind their shack of a house.

But others had seen them at one time or another and those who believed the accounts figured they'd seen forerunners – though strictly speaking, forerunners usually come in human form, or an animal, like a white moose or a wolf or the like. Anyway, since such sightings were often followed by an unexpected death in the area, and since Old Mrs. Ross saw the twin fireballs just before there were two deaths, most of the older folks were on board with the forerunner theory.

Truth be told, there's no one but old folks around here, and they're dying off pretty regular – more deaths than fireballs, if anyone was counting – so I don't personally put much stock in the explanation.

It's not something you dare take a negative stand on, for fear of being labelled, but second sight is something that people hereabouts still take to heart. Between you and me, folks around here used to believe in faeries too, and changelings – superstitions brought over from the Scottish Highlands by our Gaelic grandmothers. It's hard to take them seriously.

Kenny McIntosh didn't. Didn't take them seriously, that is. He was respectful, but he was passionate about getting to the bottom of things. And he never gave up easily. Like I said, he wrote three entire books. He was always writing to the newspapers about one thing or another, taking the time to explain something careful-like when he talked real slow to you.

I remember one time he explained that the marble inside our mountain of the same name was one end of a seam which the other end comes out in Spain. Not many folks bought that one, but a few were convinced because Kenny said it was so. Another time, or maybe the same time, he explained that the marble wasn't rock like regular rock, but the shells of tiny sea creatures from before the dinosaurs, piled up and compressed by a billion years of sediment and earthquakes. Rocks from fish somehow seems a stretch to me.

Kenny had an explanation about the fireballs, which in itself seemed odd to me – odd that he had a theory about it, I mean. I'd have thought he wouldn't believe anyone saw fire in the sky at all. But he liked to get to the bottom of things, just so he could understand them and explain to others.

Swamp gas. That's what Kenny put it down to. Escaped pockets of gas from rotten wood and vegetables in the sediment at the bottom of swamps and marshes. Look at peat, he'd say. Peat is rotted vegetation – right, vegetation, not vegetables – grown over and compressed for a few million years. It would have been turned to coal if left for 200 million years.

I couldn't help but wonder what my granddad's wooden wagon was going to be in 200 million years. He drove it accidentally into the swamp back of The Landing while hauling a keg from Old Man Ross's. When he used to tell the story, he said that it took what seemed like forever to decide between saving the horse and saving the whisky – the horse was making a terrible racket, so he had to save it and leave the whisky. "Might 'a been different if I'd had my rifle," he'd say, but I never took that too seriously.

I bet the local whisky would flame up pretty good if sparked. Maybe there's something to that, but I never mentioned it to Kenny. If it was so, he'd have to prove it himself.

Swamp gas might have explained a few other mysteries too – maybe. Lots of folks see lights in the woods where no one lives; horses get spooked for no apparent reason; a dog is suddenly frothing at the mouth; the odd dead bird on the back porch; the night an Italian road crew almost burned down the schoolhouse.

Things like that would have made investigations more useful, in my opinion, but Kenny seldom spent time on them. He preferred to set his teeth on more scientific problems. So, like I said, it seemed strange to me that he would tackle the fireballs issue. I guess since one possibility, floated by Dodger, the village drunk, was space ships filled with Martians. Kenny felt he should make a contribution. He knew a few things about space. Unfortunately, most folks around here are rather more practical, and while they were pretty resourceful problem solvers, there weren't many book-smart people Kenny could compare notes with.

∞∞

Out of frustration, and out of ideas, Kenny decided he should enlist a fellow scientist. He'd outline the problem and offer his hypothesis in hopes of getting to the bottom of it. But who to enlist? They had to be among the finest of minds – someone extremely logical, and preferably someone who understood the properties of light, if not of swamps.

Kenny was an avid reader and liked newspapers from faraway places. In those newspapers, he often read about the achievements of one of the world's leading lights of the times: Nikola Tesla. A Serbian-born inventor, Mr. Tesla lived in the Boston States where he made quite a name for himself – partly for his inventions, and partly for his flame buoyant personality.

Kenny had read a number of Mr. Tesla's articles and was quite impressed with the scope of the man's interests and abilities. So he wrote and invited the inventor to come to Cape Breton and investigate the fireballs with him. If you don't understand why on earth someone with Tesla's stellar reputation, and an ego to match, would consider such a trip, then you don't understand Kenny McIntosh; he could be very persuasive.

And you might wonder why he didn't just reach out to one of the other leading lights of the time who were already here, like Alexander Graham Bell or Guglielmo Marconi. He had thought of them, apparently, especially Bell, a Scot (though not a Highlander) who spent much of his time just down the loch, in Baddeck. But Bell was preoccupied with flying his aeroplane and giant kites. As for Marconi, well he wasn't around all that much, what with winning the Nobel Prize and all. He'd spent quite a bit of time in Cape Breton, down in Glace Bay, but his technology had outgrown the need for his physical presence there.

I don't think Kenny ever met either Marconi or Bell – though I wouldn't have put it past him – but he had read enough about Mr. Tesla to know that he'd likely jump at the chance to make a big discovery of his own, right under the noses of Bell and Marconi. His own nose was apparently out of joint because he knew his inventions were miles, and years, ahead of Marconi. It should have been him with the Nobel Prize.

So, Kenny, being a published scientist himself, put his best foot forward and wrote to Nikola Tesla to invite him to visit Cape Breton and, hopefully, to see firsthand the mysterious lights in the skies over the loch.

"Dear Mr. Tesla," Kenny's letter began, "I know you to be a man of exceptionally keen discernment...."

He was foxy about the invitation. Kenny knew that Mr. Tesla was trying to achieve the wireless transmission of electricity, and that he had succeeded in that on a small scale. But he had run into trouble trying to scale it up and, as we say in Cape Breton, was sort of between jobs. So Kenny referred to the fireballs as flashes of energy, hoping Mr. Tesla's interest would be sparked.

Kenny also knew something of Mr. Tesla's other interests. He, Mr. Tesla, was convinced that earth was being visited by intelligent beings from outer space – by aliens. In fact, he was convinced that he was in communication with aliens who gave him some of his ideas for inventions while he slept. This is probably one of the things that made people regard Mr. Tesla with some doubt, if not outright suspicion.

Interestingly, though, around this time there were a number of reports in faraway places of people seeing unidentifiable flying objects, including lights and fireballs in the skies, and of close encounters with aliens. "Little green men" were making their debut in popular culture in places as far-flung as France, Italy and the Boston States. People who study such things tried to point out that our civilization was undergoing rapid technological transformations – telephones, wireless, automobiles, flying machines – and at such times people get anxious and even irrational. Among their fears is suspicion of strangers. People of the loch were no different, including in The Landing.

There were already aliens of a sort in the area. In recent years, the longstanding limestone quarry at Marble Mountain had been purchased by the same company that ran the steel mills in Sydney and Sydney Mines. The mine output increased thanks to technology and an influx of workers with foreign accents – Italians, Poles, Swedes and Jamaicans among them.

Sometimes people fear change; sometimes they embrace it. Kenny McIntosh was one of the latter, but he wasn't above capitalizing on the fears of the former to make a point and to see something positive come of it. He worked local talk of aliens into his letter to Mr. Tesla, and that did the trick.

∞∞

It's no easy trip to get to The Landing from the Boston States – from anywhere, really. But sure enough Mr. Tesla got off the train at West Bay Road, Kenny's letter in hand, and hired a driver to take him to The Landing and to MacPhie's Carriage House. Kenny had forewarned them of the visit because he was going to be away working in Richmond County where he was under contract to survey for new roads.

I wouldn't say that Mr. Tesla fit in, exactly – quite the opposite, really – but he made himself at home while he waited for his host to return. He met some of the local colour around the village, no doubt attracting quite a bit of attention on account of his fancy dress and his accent. People around here were getting accustomed to accents because of the mine at Marble Mountain, but were unaccustomed to New York fashion.

During his encounters with local men at the ferry wharf, Mr. Tesla learned about the mining activity at Marble Mountain, and, with nothing else on his agenda just yet, one day he decided to make the trip to see for himself.

He must have been quite the sight, his fancy New York style and regal bearing in dramatic contrast with the necessarily rough and dirty activity around him at The Landing's ferry wharf, as he waited for the *Richmond* to be loaded and cast off for Marble Mountain and parts beyond. As he was apparently a friend of Kenny McIntosh, people did their best to make him feel welcome (just not too welcome, if you know what I mean). For Mr. Tesla's part, having been stung by lack of appreciation for his many talents back in the States, he was for the moment content to remain aloof and to admire the passing shoreline of the loch as the steamer made its way to Marble Mountain.

The scene there was impressive in those days. Viewed from the deck of the approaching ferry, the waterfront looked like a colony of ants had mastered the human-scale art of construction and were scurrying about in organized chaos. In the midst of the confusing array of trusses and trestles, there was a wharf for the day-to-day comings and goings of all manner of craft and people. A second rather rickety looking wharf was overshadowed by a trestle conveying limestone from the quarry that loomed over the dusty town to a waiting barge.

Large buildings, stores, churches, houses and acrid smoke contributed to the din and dirt that spoke – shouted, really – of industry and prosperity. Mr. Tesla fixed his gaze on the dark maw of a shaft into the depths of the mountain just above the high water mark, through which tons of stone steadily appeared from the darkness and dropped with a dry roar into the hold of another waiting barge.

Without going up to the site, he had no way of knowing just how deep into the earth the mine's vertical shaft was actually cut, but lack of information had never stopped his imagination before. His gaze went from the steel tower over workings that were obscured from his view, to the top of the despoiled mountain behind, and back to the empty expanse of Loch Bras d'Or behind him.

Mr. Tesla was blessed with an uncanny ability to visualize solutions to problems and to make mental maps he could later recall in detail. He used that gift to invent things that no one even knew they needed. What he saw at Marble Mountain was a comparatively obscure industrial complex blessed with naturally precipitous elevation and its own power generation. Obviously, in a sparsely populated rural setting on the shore of a large inland sea, it was just the cure he needed for his recent humiliation in the States.

Having run out of capital and time, Mr. Tesla had been forced to abandon his experiments which, by the way, included a high tower over a deep shaft into the earth. Now, here he was, in Cape Breton, where there appeared to be a plentiful supply of hungry labourers of questionable intelligence – meaning not too many questions – and, if industrial activity was any indication of prosperity, probably reasonable prospects for capital, all far from the prying eyes of New York business journalists.

All the positives aside, however industrious the mine site, the entire area was irresolvably backward, lacking one key ingredient to Mr. Tesla's needs – electricity. He must have wondered in what century he'd landed. It would take some innovation to overcome but, like I said, the inventor was not lacking in, well, invention. If the mine could operate all that equipment with steam power, it could easily generate lots of electricity. Mr. Tesla resolved to make a pitch to bring electric power to Marble Mountain.

∞∞

Kenny McIntosh was pleased as punch to have someone like Nikola Tesla to chum around with and to share his ideas, research and discoveries with. He was as anxious to learn about Mr. Tesla's research as he was to talk about his own. The two of them spent hours at a stretch in a corner of the general store hunched over complicated-looking diagrams that to anyone else looked impossible from any viewpoint.

But they made sense to those two, and the more time they spent together the more their friendship grew, to the extent that Kenny offered to help Mr. Tesla find the capital, materials and labour to generate the electricity needed to recreate his New York power plant and tower right here in Cape Breton.

Kenny was interested – fascinated – by Mr. Tesla's promise that he could transmit electricity without wires. Imagine the savings to be had if developers didn't have to erect poles and run wires. A man could live or have a business almost anywhere, he promised his investors – anywhere.

On one hand, Kenny could see the benefits of such a service; on the other hand, he made a pretty good living surveying for the roads that connected people and communities. And he would probably do alright by the erection of the hundreds, no thousands, of power poles that would be needed to bring the area fully into the 20th century. It was an exciting new vision. Kenny McIntosh, assisted by the great Nikola Tesla, would bring electricity to The Landing and Marble Mountain.

But they did not, unfortunately, fully share their respective inner visions and motivations for the project. Just as unfortunately, their respective visions were quite different.

Their plan was the talk of the whole area – mostly skeptical talk, mind you, even when shipments of large machinery started to arrive. Kenny still wanted to get to the bottom of the whole fireballs thing, but he respected the way Mr. Tesla's mind worked and came to admire the plans the inventor was hatching. He just let him get on with it.

Later, once Mr. Tesla had worked out the bugs and perfected his generators, Kenny figured he could swing their attention back around to his problem and possible explanations. Together, then, they would work on his theory that the fireballs were in fact bursts of marsh gas somehow combusted by a yet-to-be-determined source. But first things first. First, Mr. Tesla's transmissions of electricity through the air. Then, Kenny's study of the gases.

As mentioned, those two had other, different and so far unaddressed, motivations. Mr. Tesla was out to save the world. He didn't say that out loud too often on account of the reaction he sometimes got when he was a bit, shall we say, overconfident. His invention of wireless electricity – at least in theory, for it's not really an invention until you get it working – was downright utopian. Cheaper electricity for everyone. But let us not forget Mr. Tesla's other fascination – according to him we are regularly being visited by beings from outer space. I'd call them aliens, but wouldn't want to confuse them with the aliens of the human kind who were in the area at the time.

Anyway, Kenny should have remembered – but either didn't, or forgot, or chose to ignore – this side of the inventor's research interests. It might have put some distance between them.

∞∞

One day while down at the wharf catching up on the local news – and while Mr. Tesla was down the loch at the Marble Mountain site for a few days overseeing the assembly of his generator – Kenny learned that folks in the Lime Hill area had seen a number of fireballs a couple of nights before. So far as was known, not everyone saw multiple examples, but several saw at least one, and of course speculation in The Landing was ripe with suspense over whom among them were soon to die.

That kind of talk didn't go far with Kenny, but the fresh burst of atmospheric activity got him more fired up to search for an answer. Each morning brought new reports of new sightings, and people were understandably nervous, given that the number of sightings was fast approaching the total number of people still living. Kenny decided to gather a little more data so he could graph it out on paper and review things in a scientific manner.

Tethering the tools of his trade to his pack horse, Kenny set off toward Dundee, from where he intended to use his surveying equipment to map the locations of any fireballs he'd hopefully witness in the skies between The Landing and Lime Hill. That was the stretch with the greatest number of reports over the years.

Stars were just beginning to reveal themselves as twilight gave way to darkness, when he was rewarded with his first sighting – just over West Bay Marshes by his reckoning. Raising an old sextant from his father's days at sea, Kenny set his sights on the general area, hoping for another burst in the coming hours.

He wasn't disappointed. Barely able to contain himself, he recorded the bearings of a second appearance in his logbook. Then, boom! – more the sound of a spark, really – another fireball, this one farther down the loch. Then, snap!– another, this one over The Landing. And another.

Dumbfounded at his luck, Kenny noted the bearings with a shaky hand, hyperaware of the night skies over his beloved loch and the mysteries they only occasionally revealed until now. Finally, his first firsthand sightings. He'd seen the Northern Lights; he'd seen and withstood lightning storms; he'd witnessed the untimely explosion of a whisky still; he'd witnessed the glow of countless sunrises and sunsets, and he'd seen the hazy glow of distant forest fires. But he'd never before been privileged to see whatever this was.

He felt at once blessed and perplexed as he worked his way along the darkened road that he himself had mapped out many years ago. He knew the area as well as anyone, and he would use that knowledge to isolate the phenomenon he had now witnessed and, he promised himself, he would get to the bottom of it.

First light found Kenny tramping purposefully toward The Marshes, leading his pack horse bearing his equipment. His line of work is too complicated for me to relate for you, not because you wouldn't understand, but because I don't. It's all relative, apparently, though for me it's a distant relative. Anyway, I'm just here to give voice to the story as I learned it.

Once Kenny had his bearings verified and mapped out, he set about examining the terrain in hopes of formulating better hypotheses than he'd had to date, and of course, laying it out for Mr. Tesla to review.

Where was Tesla anyway? What could be so difficult or interesting to keep him holed up at Marble Mountain for so long?

∞∞

After a couple of days of stifling his excitement, and with his data nicely mapped out on paper, Kenny caught the *Richmond* for Marble Mountain intending to seek out the overdue inventor. Enquiring at the hotel on arrival Kenny learned by means of a nod and a shake of the head in the direction of the mine above the town that Mr. Tesla was holed up in an old foreman's shed above the back side of the quarry. By implication of that shake of the head, Kenny sensed that the shine was wearing off Mr. Tesla's star along with the welcome that locals had earlier shown him.

It was dusk by the time Kenny located the shack, its door open to the swarm of black flies that had followed him up from the village. Stepping into the door space, he knocked on the frame. When his eyes adjusted to the darkness, he could distinguish the outline of a long counter displaying a variety of dials and switches dimly lit by a window overlooking the quarry, and beyond it the loch. Opposite, he could make out a bench or bunk from which emanated the unmistakable sounds of someone in a deep and noisy sleep.

Kenny knocked again which brought a startled Nikola Tesla to his feet. Jumping up like that, from prone to perpendicular in an instant, caused the man to almost as quickly crumple to the floor, his head taking an awful hit off the counter on the way down. Kenny thought he'd killed him, but after a few seconds the inventor stirred and swore, probably, extending his arm in a plea for an assist to his feet, which Kenny obliged. He was taken aback by the stench off the man, who – one hand gripping Kenny's shoulder – was trying vainly to mitigate the wrinkles in his New York suit.

Kenny was no teetotaller, and he was used to seeing fellows on the dark end of a bender, but he was shocked aback at seeing this man in that condition. Feeling a little embarrassed for him, Kenny averted his eyes to survey the interior of the shack while his friend tried to compose himself.

In a curious juxtaposition, there was a confusing array of gauges, switches and wires on one side of the hut, while an assortment of kettles, jars and tubing occupied the other. Kenny recognized the paraphernalia as a whisky still. Giving Mr. Tesla the benefit of the doubt – given that the product of the still was matured enough to have laid him out – Kenny figured the shack had been used for that purpose before its latest occupant had moved in.

If Kenny wasn't entirely clear on what to do next, Mr. Tesla made it easier for him by suddenly bolting for the door and the shrubs behind the shack. The retching noises coming from the inventor's last known position had the effect of calming Kenny down a bit. By the time Mr. Tesla returned, Kenny was almost empathetic.

Almost. His Presbyterian upbringing insisted upon a measure of condescension.

To distract himself from Mr. Tesla's deplorable condition, Kenny started to examine the equipment laid out on the counter, which in turn distracted his friend from his own discomfort and embarrassment. He haltingly began to explain the various components – Kenny nodding his head as he processed it all.

Has the experiment been a success, he asked? Mr. Tesla assured him that all was proceeding as it should, as he would demonstrate momentarily. But first, something to clear his head. He was trembling so badly that Kenny had to pour the man's dram for him, though he refrained from pouring one for himself, figuring that one of them at least should be fully present.

After a moment, Mr. Tesla stood, pointlessly smoothing his lapels and straightening his necktie. He lit a small lamp over the counter, by which light Kenny could see that his mentor was unshaven and sporting a black eye. Perhaps that was from the fall, or an earlier one under the influence of a black bottle, but hopefully not from a dispute with one of the locals in the village below.

"Ziss," Mr. Tesla reached forward and, brushing aside a half-eaten sausage on the counter, engaged a circuit breaker, "connects us mit ze power. Ze mine duss not use steam after dark, und they allow me use in nacht. I make power.

"Ziss," he reached for another breaker separated from the first by a large gauge, "directs power into ze tower." He gestured into the blackness outside.

"Ziss," he grasped a wooden lever and waggled it to and fro, "ziss direct deece-charge in directions."

He paused, and drained his cup, then dipped it into a bucket of water and took a long draw. Kenny waited for Mr. Tesla to make a bolt for the bushes again and was not disappointed. Well, he was disappointed, just not surprised.

The inventor returned, a little more energetic this time, and took his position in front of the counter and window. Glancing over the controls, he gave a satisfied shrug and looking at Kenny to make sure he was paying attention, he gripped the lever with his right hand while reaching for yet another breaker with his left. Kenny felt the hair on the back of his neck stand up straight and a curious tingling in his groin at the same time a loud and ominous hum filled the hut.

Crack! With a clap like thunder, the surrounding quarry lit up bright as the sun. Again, with his left hand, Mr. Tesla pointed out the window, directing Kenny's attention to what he later described as a bolt of lightning arching over the loch.

Mr. Tesla reached forward and disengaged the breaker, returning the shack to a state of surreal calm. Kenny's heart was pounding so hard he feared for a moment it would burst out of his chest like that bolt of lightning. Relieved that it hadn't, uncharacteristically giddy from what he'd just seen, and energized like he'd not felt before, Kenny grasped Mr. Tesla's arm so hard the man flinched.

"I don't yet know how make ze stream of electricity continuous," Mr. Tesla said. "But work on it. In meantime *zis*," he patted the contraption's lever, "in right hands no more wars."

Kenny must have reacted quizzically, for Mr. Tesla took the lever again and flipped it from side to side, his eyebrows raised waiting for Kenny to take his meaning. Then, without warning, he flipped the breaker again. Crack! Another bolt of energy shot out in much the same direction as the first one. Then, he redirected the

lever ever so slightly, flipped the breaker and – crack!
– another burst, this time in a heading down the loch
toward Malagawatch.

Recalling later what happened next, Kenny told others
that, all of a sudden, Mr. Tesla pointed out the window
and screamed like a man possessed.

"Indians!" Kenny later explained that "because of
his accent, I would have sworn he said Indians, but he
was yelling 'aliens!'"

"Whether he saw his own reflection in the glass, or
the whisky was playing with his mind, I don't know,"
Kenny recalled, "but the next thing I knew, he was
swinging the lever and firing repeatedly up the shore
toward Lime Hill. Bursts of lightning were rolling up
and down the loch like it was bonfire night.

"Well, son, I wasn't sure what to do next. All I
could think of was those poor superstitious fools up
and down the loch thinking it was the end of the world.

"I was a little afraid to touch him in case the
electricity was running through him, but I had to get
him away from that trigger. I pushed him hard, he
staggered backwards and onto the bunk, and I opened
the switches so as to disarm the tower. I tell you, I was
shaking like a leaf."

By the time Kenny turned around to confront him,
Mr. Tesla was snoring, sleeping the sleep of someone
who had just saved the world. Kenny let him be and,
curious to the end, got out his logbook and began making careful notes and sketches of the controls. Later,
in the pre-dawn twilight, Mr. Tesla still sleeping it off,
Kenny made his own way down the mountain to the
village and onward on foot toward The Landing, some
fourteen miles distant.

∞∞

It took a few weeks, but things returned to normal for Kenny and for his neighbours and acquaintances up and down the loch. So far as he could determine, only he and Dodger, the village drunk, had any idea of the scope of the war of the worlds played out in the skies over Loch Bras d'Or that fateful night.

Later that year, the area was rattled by an earthquake. Kenny thought nothing of it, but Dodger saw a connection between the events. No one ever listened to Dodger, especially after he suddenly became interested in reading and sharing passages from the Bible.

Fireball sightings returned to their normal infrequency, still whispered about reluctantly by the superstitious few. "Marsh gas," Kenny maintained, "and someday I'm going to prove it."

True to his nature and his word, years later Kenny screwed up his courage and wrote to a less controversial, but still a leading light of science who might be interested in getting to the bottom of it.

'Dear Mr. Einstein,' he began....

fin

THE REBELLION
(How Cape Breton got its Welcoming Reputation)

August 2020

"Is that a name from Orkney?" teased Aonghas. "I never heard of them."

Clennie, John Hugh MacLennan, looked at his friend Aonghas Fleming with serious misgivings. "Orkney – what the frig are you talking about?"

"The clan destiny. Doesn't sound Scottish to me – not even Gaelic."

Clennie was suddenly energized.

"Cheezuss, Aonghas. You're supposed to get smarter with age. I said clandestine – it means secret. I'm telling you, there's something fishy going on over there – and it's got nothing to do with fishing so don't say it."

"I'm just messin' wit' ya Clennie – I get what you're sayin'."

It was August. Aonghas's little boat was slowly trolling the loch near Campbell's Island, where an old resort was being rejuvenated – lately the talk of everyone up and down the shore. All last winter, truckload after truckload of building materials were driven across the ice to the island that shelters The Landing from the sometimes tumultuous waves of Loch Bras d'Or.

It was obvious that they were renovating the sprawling timber lodge and assorted cabins strung along the crescent beach of Coral Cove, as it's known. It's not coral, of course, but the sand is so fine and white, and the water so blue-green under a cloudless sky, you could be forgiven for thinking it was tropical.

The lodge in question was originally built about a hundred years ago as a retreat for wealthy Americans.

Campbell's Island is an island within an island – Cape Breton Island. Cape Breton juts out into the Atlantic Ocean like a severed appendage of Nova Scotia. It's politically a part of that Province yet culturally distant. It's the kind of place anthropologists dream of, if only it were inhabited by some overlooked civilization.

Actually, at one time it was just that. Cape Breton was inhabited for millennia by the Mi'kmaq, the Indigenous peoples of the region – who were very civilized, thank you very much, living quite prosperously and peacefully before Europeans came. About 400 years ago, they were joined by some French, then a small bunch of adventurous Lowland Scots who thought they owned the place. Then a different sort of French who thought that *they* owned the place; then the English who set about trying to prove that *they* owned it.

The French and English fought tooth and nail over the territory – less than amusing and no doubt confusing to the Mi'kmaq. But once the European political situation stabilized somewhat, everyone settled down and got back to ignoring Cape Breton – and the Mi'kmaq. Shiploads of displaced Gaelic-speaking Highland Scots started arriving, looking for a little peace and quiet from their aristocratic tormentors back across the Atlantic.

Cape Breton wasn't the first choice for many Scots coming in the late 18th and early 19th centuries. They mostly went to Nova Scotia and Prince Edward Island and only when all the good bottom lands were sewn up did they start to settle in Cape Breton – then they multiplied by the tens of thousands. For more than a hundred years, Scots-Gaelic was a predominant language and culture hereabouts, including on Campbell's Island, believe it or not. How the heck families who steaded out on that island kept themselves alive and growing in the days before outboard motors is a mystery to the present generation.

Anyway, that was about 200 years ago. More to the point of this story, before the First World War, a few wealthy Americans who had invested in the great limestone quarry at Marble Mountain, just down the road from The Landing, saw it as a place for their rich friends to vacation. Then, after the war, the lodge was used to escape the flu epidemic for a few weeks or months at a time. It lasted quite a while because then rich folks escaping the depression of the Great Depression kept it in business until the Second World War.

Lately, as Clennie and Aonghas could clearly see from their vantage point, the place was coming alive yet again.

"There's van-loads of tourists coming from the airport every month or so," Clennie said unnecessarily. "Clean vans with tinted windows."

"I seen them, Clennie," said Aonghas, reeling in his line to see if the bait still looked appetizing.

"Boats coming and going between The Landing and the resort all friggin' night," said Clennie.

"I hear them, Clennie."

"They hired that German sausage maker over in Malagawatch to roast a pig on the beach."

"I smelled it, Clennie."

"Aonghas, get the net."

"You planning to catch one, Clennie?"

"No, shit-for-brains, I got a fish on."

Aonghas picked up the fishing net and went to the side of the boat to assist. "They're starting to run, Clennie," he said as he brought a smallish mackerel into the boat between them. "We'll eat tonight buddy!"

"My sister's boy, Angus Beag, says it's a school, or a conference centre."

Aonghas stood up straight and pretended to scan the bay. "I don't see Little Angus anywhere, Clennie. How's he know the mackerel's schooling?" He loved to get Clennie going when he was fired up about something.

"Not the mackerel, fish of a different colour, tourists. He sees them in the computer. He says people come to listen to speeches by some professor."

"What in the name of the almighty would possess them people to come all this way for speeches? Don't they get enough at home?"

"Beats me Aonghas. Angus Beag says it's mostly politics. He says that the leader – the professor – is some kind of expert on motivation—"

"An engineer?" asked Aonghas.

"Not locomotion, Aonghas, motivation, the political kind. Anyway, it sounds like these folks don't like the way things is going in the States after losing two elections in a row; they're holding meetings and doin' their bitchin' down here so they don't call attention to themselves up there."

"There's been plenty of Americans coming here for years, Clennie, Germans too," Aonghas pointed out. "Some of them have fit in pretty good, those who want to. The others pretty much keep to themselves, which is okay by me. They're only here for a week or two anyways, most of 'em. They don't go to church. You never see or hear of them except during the Celtic Colours."

"There's Americans, and there's Americans, Aonghas. But it seems different this time. There's more and more, and something don't seem right. And haven't they been buying up all kinds of property hereabouts! They says there's a hundred lots in that new subdivision past the mountain."

"What's wrong with their own places? Why do they need to be driving up our taxes and such?"

"Little Angus – Angus Beag – says that the leader's computer page complains about the way things is being run by the Democrats. Too many rules, too much Socialism, and too many immigrants, he says."

"So because he don't like immigrants there, he wants to be one here? In Cape Breton? Makes no sense to me."

"You have a point, there Aonghas. Besides, there's plenty of rules here too."

∞∞

The cheque-day social club in the Tanneries Tavern rarely solves the world's problems, but the retired men who ration out their allowances there one afternoon a week give the world a thorough going over anyway. Most weeks they each nurse their budgeted single beer over an entire afternoon, but when the pension cheques come in the purse strings loosen a bit, as do their collective imaginings and opinions.

Opinions here are as virulent and as varied as the clouds that alternately race, roar and rain over The Landing on any given day – opinions and tales as tall as the Caledonia pines that dwarf the vintage shingled homes overlooking the loch.

There's no particular protocol for the meetings – a complete stranger in this strange land could sit in and easily follow the conversation, if not the reasoning, and perhaps even offer an opinion, if they were inclined. In the old days, folks hereabouts conducted such klatches in the old general store in the old way – in the Gaelic – but even the old-timers who grew up in Gaelic-speaking households now converse in the English.

Fewer and fewer people speak more than a few pat phrases in their grandparents' tongue – and those just for show, especially during tourist season. The loss of the Gaelic surely had a lot to do with the problems of the whole world being mostly in English.

On this particular cheque day, Hamish MacKay, Daniel Ross, Aonghas Fleming, Marshall Rimbeau and Roddy MacLean were settling in for an afternoon of good-natured insults and tall tales. Hamish comes from one of the oldest families hereabouts, though almost everyone makes the same claim. Marshall Rimbeau was the only one who could legitimately say so.

Rimbeau's friends called him Rambo because of his prodigious size and because he was almost always dressed in camouflage. "Camo" clothing is a common fashion in rural Cape Breton, but Rambo takes it to extremes. His mother is Mi'kmaq; his father is from one of the oldest Acadian families in Nova Scotia. Hunting and fishing played a major role in his life.

"I hear they found another one last night, Hamish," said Daniel Ross. His sister's boy was in the West Bay Road Volunteer Fire Department, so Daniel had lots of third-hand knowledge about local emergencies, rescues and the like.

"That's the third one on the mountain road this year." Hamish MacKay shook his head in disgust.

"You'd think anyone smart enough to drive their computerized car all this way would look out the window while they're doing it," agreed Daniel. "Those GDS's is no good when it comes to local roads. Or one of those new subdivision roads not on the maps yet."

"GPS," corrected Hamish. "Global Positioning Systems."

"GDS is what I call them," Daniel replied. "God damn senseless. If your Korean rent-a-car uses a Japanese computer, and an Yankee map, on a Cape Breton road that leads you straight up a friggin' mountain path that would cripple a goat, wouldn't you think something was up? Down?" He slapped his knee to punctuate his little joke.

∞∞

The trouble with coming in on the middle of a conversation is that you lose precious time catching up so you can get your oar in. It came as no surprise that, arriving a little late, Clennie MacLennan jumped in to the conversation on roads without knowing the context.

"I'm telling you Hamish, if I see that friggin' Tory in at Sobeys, I'm going to give him a piece of my mind." Any mention of local road conditions – which were, in a word, deplorable most of the year, decrepit the rest of the time – always got Clennie going.

"What is wrong with this province when we can't even get decent roads in an election year!" he continued. "What the Cheezuss are we votin' for?"

"We were talking about Campbell Road, up the mountain," said Daniel. "Hamish here says there was another family of tourists stranded up there on account of their GDS."

"GPS," Hamish said again.

"If my taxes go up any more, it'll put me and my mother into the poorhouse," said Roddy MacLean, throwing in with Clennie. "The taxes keep going up while services go down – it's not right."

"'Dey say," Marshall Rimbeau interjected, "'dat your generation's de wealt'iest ever."

"Fake news, Rambo dear, fake news." Roddy patronizingly patted his large friend's nearest shoulder.

"Sure, we're rich," spat Clennie. "We got property that city folk can only dream of owning. Fact is, nobody truly wants it. That real estate fellow from Hawkesbury tells me I could list our place for ten times what I paid for it."

"You never paid for that place anyway," objected Aonghas. "You took it over from your father when your brother wasn't looking."

"Assets aren't cash." Roddy MacLean savoured his lager for effect. "Those MacIsaacs over in Black River, the ones who retired and bought their grandparents' old homestead back from that German couple? They have to sell the house 'cause they can't afford both heat and taxes – that's rich."

Ignoring the snipe at his home ownership, Clennie did what every argumentative Canadian does; he blamed it on Americans.

"Mark my words," he urged. "The big auto makers don't make cars anymore – only trucks and SUVs. And what's the best way to hurry up the process and get us all into those more expensive rigs? Bad roads."

Clennie paused so his audience could consider this latest conspiracy and argue with him. With nothing forthcoming, he enlightened them further. "If everybody's got a truck, the roads don't need to be smooth, and they save money on pavement. The more expensive everyone's ride gets, the more taxes they collect. The bigger the trucks, the more gas and the more taxes roll in. The more expensive some things gets, the more expensive everything else gets.

"Of course, bigger vehicles and more gas burned mean more climate change, and that'll mean more and bigger bridges to carry bigger trucks – and more engineers – over wider spans. We're in a bad way, men."

"It's like we're all in a giant game of musical chairs," said Professor Jim Gregory, as he took his customary seat. "I heard Maude Barlow explain it that way. We're all marching happily in circles to someone else's tune. But when the music stops, there aren't enough seats for everyone, and the slower ones to react – usually the poorer or undereducated – are left out. Again. We all keep playing the game, and the same ones keep calling the tune."

The analysis was met with blank looks and silence. Clennie took it upon himself to get things back on track. His track.

"Joe Abbass has approval for another subdivision," he said, which everyone knew already. "Another hundred building lots at $100,000 each – another hundred mansion hideaways for another hundred millionaires to hide out for a week or two in summer. It's not right."

"Good construction jobs," Aonghas pointed out. "My sister's girl is plumbing three different houses right now, and plenty more to come. They're something to see, she says."

"It's good for the County's tax base," Roddy noted. "No wonder they don't say nothing. And God knows no one else has made use of that land, not since before the war."

"Doan forget, 'dat lan' – 'dis lan' – were stole from my people," said Rimbeau.

"It wouldn't be too bad, having a few more people living here," said Clennie thoughtfully, looking around the room. "But they don't really want to *live* here, do they? They pretty much keep to themselves."

"And temporary jobs don't put kids through college," noted Daniel, "though God knows Cape Bretoners know how to drag things out to advantage." Everyone knew that to be true. He was thoughtful for a moment as he sipped his pint. "But there is something different about this latest bunch."

"I'm telling you, they are up to no good." Clennie, happy that the conversation was coming round to this matter, began recounting a litany of clues that the next American Revolution was being planned right here on the west bay of Loch Bras d'Or: exclusive meetings, wild accusations and conspiracy theories on the Internet, and van-loads of tourists who don't seem too interested in acting like tourists.

"It's a free country, Clennie," said Jim Gregory. "What do we care if a few opinionated tourists want to whisper their suspicions into their Sam Adams around the campfire."

Jim Gregory wasn't a local in a local understanding of what is local, but he'd lived here long enough that folks were used to having him around. A retired professor from the Catholic university on the Mainland, and an American dual citizen, Professor Jim, as these fellows knew him, sometimes even helped make sense of things – sometimes.

"Look," he continued, which made Clennie stiffen as if to do battle for control of the conversation. "My reading of Cape Breton history is that these things run in cycles. People come. Some stay. Some move on. It won't last."

Clennie scoffed, but brought himself up short, and didn't interupt.

"Think about it," the professor continued. "Give or take a decade or so, there's not much here now, but a hundred years ago industrialization and coal brought people and prosperity. Did it last? No.

"A hundred years before that, it was the Gaels. Gaelic was the second-most spoken language here. A hundred years befor that, the French at Louisbourg. A hundred years before that, the French colonized mainland Nova Scotia."

"Us Acadians," acknowledged Rimbeau.

"Right," Professor Jim continued. "A hundred years before that – still more French. See? It doesn't last."

"And the Chinese," Clennie added knowlingly. To the blank stares he went on to remind them of the not-so-recent book that insisted the Chinese had a city on Kelly's Mountain, in the 1420s.

"That theory was refuted with some certainty by historians and archaeologists alike," Professor Jim reminded them. "But that reminds me to add Henry St. Clair around the same time, and even the Norse – Erikson – before that."

Evcryonc gave silent consideration to the professor's little history lesson until Clennie cleared his throat to break the silence. Though not before Aongus offered his summary.

"So this too shall pass," he said. "We just have to outlive 'em."

To this Rombeaud added, with a smile, "from your lips to de Creator's ear. My people keep hoping, Aongus, we keep hoping."

Clennie struck a conspiratorial pose. "What if they're plotting something big, like 9/11?" Now he had their attention. He leaned back and let that sink in.

"Cheezuss, Clennie," Hamish interjected. "That one was hatched right under their noses – why the hell would anyone go to all the trouble and expense of coming over *here* to start a war over *there*?"

"Their leader, that professor fellow – not you Jim – has had a summer place down here for years now. Even got a road named after him. Well, Angus Beag says he loves to play up to Republicans and Tories who, as we all know, hate Democrats and liberals and can't stand their President.

"They come down here so they can hang out with people who think the same and speak the same. Then they write letters and make little videos saying things they'd be in trouble for sayin' up there. They hate the President even more than their government and will say and do just about anything to get their way in the next election."

"People can think and say what they want here, Clennie, it's a free country," Professor Jim pointed out.

"Clennie says it's the Klan," Aonghas snickered.

Professor Jim turned quickly, and incredulously, toward Clennie, his eyebrows raised in silent questioning – whether of the accusation or of the sanity of the accuser didn't much matter.

"Cheezuss, Aonghas, clan, not The Klan," Clennie corrected quickly. "I said clandestine." Turning to Professor Jim, he asked, "I don't think that's even allowed here, is it? The Ku Klux Klan?"

Daniel weighed in. "Maybe you're right, Clennie – I mean, wrong. The President hates the Klan, and the Klan hates the President. Maybe a bunch of them are buying up property thinking nobody will notice or care."

This wasn't quite what Clennie had in mind, but seeing as the concept of a secret society was catching a wave, he stayed that course.

"It's not right. We have laws. People like that shouldn't be allowed to stir up trouble – they could get us all in trouble."

"I don't know," cautioned Daniel. "How much trouble? It's not like they're going to train a little army or start launching rockets."

Clennie was suddenly wide-eyed. "Sweet Cheezuss! That's it! The space port! The rocket-launching pad they're trying to build over in Canso!"

He actually had everyone's attention – and without any of the usual eye-rolling or tongue-clucking just yet.

"Don't you see? It's not to launch rockets into outer space. It's to launch rockets into the Boston States!" Clennie sat back, greatly inflated by his revelation and by the silence of his audience, which he perceived as respectful. It was Aonghas who spoke first.

"You know," he started quietly, "there's another reason we should do something about this. Let's say what Clennie says is true – not the rockets, or that the clan is growing—"

"I never said clan!" Clennie insisted again.

Aonghas continued. "Let's say there's enough of them that people do start to notice and start to investigate. The authorities might be all over this place – like spies to honey." He paused to let the others catch up. Seeing only blank looks, he continued, only more slowly.

"Secret Service. Police. Detectives. Agents." He emphasized the 'A' for effect: 'A A-gents.' "Driving up and down the road. Walking through the woods. All hours of the day. The night."

Hamish was first to catch on.

"Cheezuss!" he exclaimed. "The *uisge!*"

Roddy's complexion got blotchy suddenly, as he simultaneously paled and blushed.

Aonghas took on a knowing look, as he sat back and sipped of his pint.

Daniel sat up straight, so did Professor Jim. The latter preferred his whisky to come from licensed and inspected distillers, but he did make his own wine and understood the need to economize. Though output had declined in direct proportion with the population decline, the local stuff was of legendary quality and commanded respect. Clennie liked to refer to it as artisanal.

Backwoods manufacturing and agriculture had changed in recent years; a new generation of locals was applying what they learned from distilling grain and making wines to other, shall we say, "other crops." There were more than grapes and grains growing in the upslope breezes on Roddy's grandparents' near-abandoned farm high above the loch.

"Gentlemen." Clennie, puffed up to make an announcement, put down his pint purposefully. "It's our patriotic duty to take action."

The others, except Professor Jim, muttered in what Clennie imagined to be agreement, so he continued.

"Our way of life must be protected," he said. "So, what now, Professor?"

Jim Gregory raised an eyebrow. "What the Jesus do you need me for?"

"You're the doctor here. And you're one of them. American, I mean. There's Americans and there's Americans. Wasn't I just saying that to Aonghas the other day. Maybe you could speak to them, find out what's really going on."

With all eyes upon him, Professor Jim couldn't help but think the ask was a bit much. Active in the community – the church, the garden club, the beautification committee, the "Save Our Post Office" committee – he sometimes felt that it was his chequebook that had citizenship rather than he and his family. In retirement, at times he took part in social conversations feeling not so much included as needed.

"I'm not, as you say it, 'one of them'. I share birthright to be sure, but not much else, and in case you haven't noticed, I don't often mix with my countrymen."

"Persons," said Hamish. Then, in answer to the questiong looks, "you said 'countrymen,' isn't it country persons?"

Aonghas took over. "You speak their language, Jim. You still have an accent. How long have you lived here?"

"Forty years."

"Forty years!" Hamish exclaimed. "Do you think you'll get to like it here?" His grin revealed the true nature of the question.

"We do like it here. Our children grew up here. If they have children, we hope they too will grow up here."

"God knows we need a few youngsters around here," said Hamish. "This place is dyin'."

Aonghas took over again. "Tell me Jim – how is it you came, stayed and became almost like one of us? Your countrymen don't do that. The majority anyway. Why d'you suppose that is?"

"Well—"

"Maybe you could find out what's going on out there." Hamish tipped his head in the general direction of Campbell's Island.

"I don't really want to be involved with them," the professor replied. "We don't share the same views of the world."

"Ah, you *do* know something," said Clennie, hoping to steer the conversation toward greater clarity. "What's goin' on, and what should we do about it?"

"Reinstate the toll booth at the Causeway," suggested Daniel. "That'll weed out some of them."

"That would hurt us more than the tourists," replied the professor.

"Well, we can't close the Causeway, and we can't build a wall. The flu epidemic didn't change things. For every American who stayed home like they were supposed to, there were two coming here thinking they could get away with it. Or get away with it. So, what's the solution perfessor?"

"Well, b'y," started the professor, slipping teasingly into vernacular observed over four decades, "for years I just thought folks from faraway places buying lots and building vacation homes were—"

"Mansions," interrupted Hamish. "Mansions on prime waterfront property driving up our taxes."

"Money to burn," Aonghas added. "Probably illegal money too."

"Mansions compared with what you and I and most others around here live in, Hamish," the professor continued, "but not compared with some of the houses where they live, though not necessarily their own. The U.S. dollar is pretty favourable against the Canadian these last few years."

"Why is that, anyway?" Hamish asked.

Ignoring the question to stay on topic, the professor continued. "As I understand them, there are a few reasons they come here. I was lucky; I came at a time when the new university needed faculty – I came for a job and fell in with you lot. Amazingly, I stayed anyway," he added with a smile. "Or maybe we couldn't see ourselves going back there, what with the George Bushes and all.

"They, on the other hand..." he gestured with his two hands as though lumping something together as he nodded toward the island.

Then, like he was engaging a group of students, he began enumerating, extending his thumb – one, "it is *so* crowded and busy where they are from; they want what we ... what *you*, have."

He extended his index finger – two, "they love telling their neighbours they have a vacation home in Nova Scotia, especially explaining where that is."

Three – "there are just too many rules and too many taxes in most states. They are starting to resent paying high taxes only to see other people benefit. They don't see things like we do here, things like health services and welfare for people who don't work or seem to work as hard as them. Funny," here he gestured with his raised thumb toward the island, "they don't notice that the rich don't pay taxes either and still get those benefits."

Four – "I think people are afraid of the future, of what's coming. Y'know – many of these people are still bemoaning the war, if you know what I mean."

"Mexico? 1812?" Hamish asked.

Clennie rolled his eyes in disgust and shook his head for emphasis. "He's talking about the Civil War, right Jim?"

"Right. I was stateside a couple of years ago, rubbing elbows with people whose world view was almost polar opposite to mine – opposite to most people's, or so I always thought."

"Ha! You're from Maine!" Hamish chortled. "What would you know about what *most* people think?"

"Very funny – coming from a backwoods bachelor from Barra," chided the professor in return. Resuming his display of four of the five fingers on his left hand, he continued. "My point is – or would have been – that out of 330-plus million Americans, even a small percentage of malcontents – complainers – can seem an overwhelming number to a small area like ours.

"One thing I *will* say, however," and here he extended his pinky finger to make point five – "is that an awful lot of the folks buying and building in these subdivisions seem to hold the same political views. People who don't like their government, and especially don't like immigrants of colour, and whose views, when they do get together, can be disquieting – disturbing – to me at least."

"Vaccines, don't forget," Daniel interjected, "they don't trust their government for anything."

Professor Jim continued. "I don't want to have those conversations so I avoid socializing with them. I prefer the company of you Scotchmen to those—"

"Republicans," Clennie chimed in.

"Not all Republicans are bad, are they Jim," Hamish stated as though he knew a few.

"And not all bad people are Republicans," the professor replied.

"So you think they're down here holding meetings and planning something?" Clennie asked no one in particular in order to keep the conversation focused. "And if they are, don't you think we should do something? We don't want the government to think we are soft on conspirators – remember how they went apeshit on law-and-order after 911?"

Aonghas had been reflective the last while, but now shifted in his seat.

"It occurs to me—" His thought was interrupted by a derisive snort from Clennie. Aonghas gave his friend an exaggerated look of hurt, and continued. "What do these people have in common? They're from different cities; they can't all know each other. How do they find out about us, about Cape Breton?"

"Some by word of mouth, undoubtedly," Professor Jim replied. "Some because they hear about these conferences—"

"Maybe they Google it," said Hamish.

"Google what?" Clennie snickered. "Clan Destiny?"

The professor continued. "Maybe some hear about these conferences and want to rub elbows with people who think the same as they do. Some see it at the trade shows the developer goes to."

"What kind of trade shows?" Clennie thought this was going in an interesting direction.

"Look here." Professor Jim had his smartphone out in pursuit of an answer. He was delicately tapping and scrolling over Google responses.

Most of the men around the table were not cell-phone users, but their children or grandchildren were, so they were not oblivious to the technology. There just wasn't good enough reception in the area to warrant such a device – not that they'd be able to manage them with any great success. To Aonghas, it looked rather elegant, as though the professor was conducting a tiny orchestra or, and closer to the truth, casting a spell.

The tavern had decent high-speed Wi-Fi. The professor leaned over so Clennie, and Aonghas beyond him could see the results of his search.

"Look here."

"Cheezuss Christmas! Look at all the guns!" Clennie shook his head in disbelief. On the professor's tiny screen, a parade of photos of guns on display at booth after booth after booth.

"About 5,000 gun shows in the U.S. every year, it says here," Professor Jim noted. "Did you know there are more guns than people in the U.S.?" Then he backed up and Googled 'Travel shows selling Canadian vacation properties.'

"That's him!" Aonghas declared, squinting over Clennie's shoulder as a photo of four men, grinning slickly for the camera, came into focus. "That's the guy giving lectures on Campbell's Island. I saw him on Angus Beag's computer. Standing right beside you-know-who," he pointed at the small screen, "Joe Abbass, the developer."

This was a revelation even for Clennie. "Well, I'll be," he said, "They're in it together."

"So what?" asked Hamish.

Clennie paused – perhaps to reflect, perhaps for effect, but his eyes lit up as an answer surfaced.

"So one can sell his land, and the other can sell his revolution." This went over the heads of the others, but Hamish reached out his hand seeking the professor's phone for a closer look.

"I seen this guy too – last week, at the hotel in town. He was herding a bunch of Americans in the lobby."

"For one of his conferences, maybe," suggested Aonghas.

"And potential land buyers, maybe," Clennie added thoughtfully. "I'm thinking the professor – not you Jim – lures unhappy rich people to his right-wing seminars out on the island and treats them to a fine time in our little paradise, boating, four-wheeling, sunset roasts.... And who just happens to have brochures handy...?"

All heads were nodding their enlightenment.

Professor Jim was looking at another photo carefully. "Is that...." His voice trailed off while he processed something. "That's Barbie! Bonnie Conroy. People called her Barbie. She was for years a commentator on CNN. She resigned in disgrace a few years ago – on the wrong side of politics, or something. I used to watch her all the time...." He looked up and quickly added "for research. Now she's a mouthpiece for Republicans. She's into conspiracy theories and such. Thinks the government and Bill Gates are in cahoots to take away everyone's guns and put mind-control computer chips in our Corn Flakes, or something like that."

"I bet she's a big draw at the conferences, TV personality and all," said Clennie. "One big happy right-wing family way down here in the Canadian north woods where no one will notice."

"And the prices!" exclaimed Hamish. "Who the hell can afford the real estate? Them people get all hyped up about their conservative colony here and buy building lots before they think things through."

"And Abbass and that professor – not you Jim – buy back the lots from the dreamers at fire-sale prices, then resell them to the next batch of losers. Sell high, buy low, sell high, eh?"

"Doan be too sure 'dat, 'Amish – 'bout bein' loser, I mean," Rambo said quietly. "It be good way to spen' money 'dat yer not s'pose to 'ave, eh? Buy 'igh, sell low, sell 'igh – repeat. Good racket."

Aonghas shifted himself a little closer. Forearms on the table, he said quietly, "Uncle Sam probably spies on them, and in all likelihood is spying on us too. In the middle. We're in a bad spot, boys. A real bad spot."

"'Dis is Canada," said Rimbeau. "'Dey are not goin' start a war. 'Dey can't bring guns wit' dem." He turned to Professor Jim. "Can 'dey?"

"Not that kind of war, Rambo" the professor replied. "Wars are not just fought with guns and bombs anymore. Wars are more often fought with words, with information – insults, interference, threats, fake news, hatred. With words you can wage war anywhere in the world, from anywhere in the world. Including Cape Breton."

"Even Malagawatch, when the Internet's working," said Clennie. "Jim's right. The situation calls for a war of words."

The professor gestured, palms outward, to put a stop to it. "Hold it right there Clennie. You're not going to be able to engage with these people on their level. No way."

"But 'dey're in Canada," Rimbeau repeated. "'Dey can't say 'tings 'ere like 'dat."

"Say what things?" shrugged the professor.

"Free speech, right Jim?" said Daniel Ross.

"We can't jes *let* 'dem say 'dem t'ings 'ere. People can' come 'ere and 'ide behind *our* free speak to cause trouble in 'deir own country.

"'Dere should be a big sign in de h'airport 'dat lists Canadian value, an' underneat' it should say 'ouse rules'."

"Cheezuss, Rambo, I get what yer saying', but it sounds an awful lot like the kind of thing they are running *from* – rules and more rules."

"Might do de trick."

"Y'know," said Professor Jim, "in a funny way, I kind of feel sorry for them – the buyers, that is."

"Don't feel sorry for millionaires," clucked Clennie. His Highland resentment of other people's success was showing through.

"Hear me out. Maybe there's an answer in here somewhere." Hands folded on the table before him,

Professor Jim closed his eyes as though he was visualizing something complex, and didn't want it confused by his surroundings.

"In a way," he said after a moment, "we have a group of unhappy people being exploited by a clever sales pitch that fools them into thinking they are able to buy their way into a private little paradise with neighbours who are just like them.

"Instead of buying into gated communities walled in by electric fences, they are walled in by acres of scrubby spruce. It's something they can't do in the back woods of their own country because they've spent 300 years marginalizing rural folks.

The professor paused; Clennie took the opportunity to get his oar in. "And how many actually do anything once they're here? How many actually build a house on land they pay a fortune for? They can't even get health care, can they?"

Professor Jim raised an eyebrow opening one eye in a bid to continue.

"Snake oil," he said. "C'mon, you have to feel sorry for someone being bilked out of their life savings on a false promise of a cure. They're victims. Well, maybe that's a stretch."

"I have a hard time feeling sorry for anyone rich *and* stupid," Clennie clucked.

"And something else," the professor continued. "When I reflect on how good this area has been to my family, to my children, I find it regrettable that those people don't mix in – don't get to know the land, or the culture, or the people."

"Well, *some* people, anyways," Hamish chimed in with a good-natured nod in Clennie's direction.

"You'll miss me when I'm gone, Hamish," bristled Clennie. Then, to the professor, "I don't believe they want to mix in, Jim. You said yourself that they want isolation, even if only for a few weeks a year."

"Seems we can't keep them out, and it's no good trying to make them feel unwelcome, because they don't want to be welcomed."

"So, let's do the opposite and see what happens. Let's make them feel *more* welcome," Aonghas offered. "Try some reach-out, like the church does."

"Outreach," professor Jim corrected absent-mindedly.

"Them people don't go to any of our churches," Clennie reminded them. "They prefer those TV-angelists."

"I said *like* church," defended Aonghas. "I didn't mean just church." He shifted in his seat to position himself more assertively. "Look. There's lots more going on around here than church. Country breakfasts. Music. Cards. Ceilidhs. Darts. Dances. Maybe there's a way to get them more interested in getting to know us."

"Show them what we're made of," offered Hamish.

"'Dat'd do it!" Rimbeau jumped in, slapping his meaty hand on the table for effect. "You'll scare 'dem away for good," he guffawed.

Grinning, Hamish retorted, "right! Introduce them to Clennie here. That'll fix 'em!"

Clennie opened his mouth as if to contribute a rebuttal, but paused, eyes narrowing as he considered his response to the teasing.

"You know," he began. He paused again.

Good-natured teasing is part of everyday male tavern talk, as everyone knows. Clennie MacLennan gives as good as he gets, and the momentary lapse in spontaneity was uncharacteristic.

More often than not, Clennie's friends and neighbours only half-listen when he speaks. They are all opinionated – a great Highland tradition – but Clennie's heightened sense of his own intelligence, while tolerated, was not taken too seriously. He tended toward conspiracies and complaints, as opposed to conversation and consensus. Unconsciously, they braced themselves for yet another issue from his bottomless well of negative opinion.

"You know," Clennie repeated. "Joking aside, Aonghas and Hamish may be on to something. Fire with fire."

He looked conspiratorially to Professor Jim and translated more assertively. "Kill 'em with kindness."

Clennie looked into the faces around the table, pausing when his eyes reached the multi-paned windows overlooking the road and, beyond that the cove, where the eastern tip of Campbell's Island calmed the choppy outer waters of the loch. The cove was as smooth as glass, reflecting the grey-blue expanse of sky and the grey-green shoreline of the south mountain beyond.

Turning himself more or less toward the professor, Clennie puffed himself up a little and began.

"Jim, you gave me as good an explanation as we've heard for your countrymen's desire to be left alone. We should honour that. But if there is an undesirable element among them, it would be unpatriotic to ignore it. We ought to do the right thing without letting them know we're onto 'em."

Aonghas said, "talk is cheap, Clennie. What d'you think we can do about it."

"Boys, I think it's time to grease up the wheels on the welcome wagon."

Pulling his chair in a little closer, Clennie outlined his plan. They would enlist every church, community group and busybody up and down the loch in an all-out social offensive. Smiles, handshakes, invites, ceilidhs, cards and casseroles. Professor Jim would offer weekly sessions explaining Cape Breton history and local culture. "CB-101," Clennie called it.

"The idea," he explained, "is to be in their face so much they either forget about their problems or head for the hills. Real estate prices will drop in no time. And taxes."

"Taxes don' go down, Clennie. 'Dey never go down." Rimbeau got up to go to the washroom, but after only a few steps he came back to the table. "I jus' had 'nudder idee, me. Remine me when I come back. Anyone wanna beer while I'm up?"

"I like that idea, Rambo dear," smiled Hamish.

"I'll take a rain check, thanks," said Aonghas, "another beer and I'd have to get Clennie here to drive me home."

"Wouldn't wish 'dat on you, Aonghas," smiled Rambo. "Professor, yes? Daniel, no? Alright 'den, I'll be right back."

When he returned and had set the beers before their intended, Rambo turned his chair around and straddled the seat so that his arms rested on the back.

"When your people came 'ere 'dey cleaned land for de farm' dat eventually line de shores of Bras d'Or from one en' to 'de odder. My h'ancestors t'ought yours might be decent neighbour and 'dere were 'nough room for everyone, and let 'dem settle in, even help 'dem. 'Dey were ahead of 'de time, my people; I like to t'ink 'dey reco'nize 'de value of diversity.

"It's ironic 'dat your people, 'de Highlanders, were run off 'de homelands by 'de h-English who 'den turned 'roun' and grant lan' – Indian lan' – to create opportunities for people 'dey din' respec'.

"Anyway, we come 'dis far and 'dere is no goin' back. But isn't it sad 'dat now 'dere's only a few of you leff, all 'dat farmland growed over? Why not put it to work again?

"Canada want immigrants. No? Yes. Why not immigrant farmers? Your ancestors din' know much about farming, and look what 'dey done. 'Magine what a experience farmer could do."

"Cheezuss, Rambo," Clennie shifted in his seat, anxious to take back control of the conversation. "What in God's name does that have to do with the revolution?"

Rimbeau held up his hand to beg for patience. "I don' preten' to know what 'dey could do in de winter, but if de gov'ment took over all 'dis overgrown farmland and offer it to farmer families from Mexico, or Sout' America, or Asia, it might bring 'dis island back to life."

"I still don—" Clennie protested.

"T'ink about it Clennie. Wha'd we say your new neighbour was running away from?" Rambo held up his hand like the professor had. "One – in no p'ticular order – democrats; two, crowds; three..."

"Immigrants!" Hamish jumped in.

"Immigrants," confirmed Rimbeau, dropping his hand.

"Immigrants," repeated Clennie. "You want Chinese farmers to live here and grow veg'tables."

"Mexicans," Daniel reminded them.

"Expecially Mexicans," Hamish emphasized. "Republicans hate Mexicans. Aonghas, what d'ye think?"

Aonghas Fleming paused in reflection before answering. "Wouldn't they find it cold?"

Hamish guffawed and clapped his friend on the back. "Warm hearts and whisky, Aonghas. Warm hearts and whisky."

Clennie wasn't so sure. "So we fill the glens with friendly Mexican farmers, and the unfriendly Americans will leave? Don't be so sure."

"Won't that have an impact on our local culture?" asked Aonghas.

"It might even strengthen it Aonghas," Hamish said. "More and more people will come out to our ceilidhs and concerts; their children will take up the fiddle, learn Gaelic and step dancing. It could turn tourists into troubadours. Their farming know-how could make the glens productive again. I like it. It's not like they'll ever outnumber us. What could go wrong?"

∞∞

Kisikewiku's – Ripening Moon (August 1820)

"They found another family of wool-wearers on the mountain yesterday." Thomas Sylliboy shook his head in disbelief. His nephew, Michael Googoo, was a forest keeper from the neighbouring summer camp at Malikewe'jk, so Thomas frequently had third-hand news of encounters with the increasing number of Scotland's people clearing plots of land and building log cabins – homesteads they called them.

"Using an English interpretation of a French map, but speaking only Gaelic," scoffed Eugene Denny. "The maps name people, instead of describing the land. How can they expect to find their way around?"

It was the second week of Kisikewiku's. Thomas and Eugene and their friends Sulian and Mas'l were gathered in Sulian's wikuom near Wiaqaji'jk, the mixing place on the west bay of Pitu'pok, Loch Bras d'Or.

"There are more and more of them," said Mas'l. "At least these Gaels respect the land. Their English masters only worked to destroy it. Those English took Unama'ki from the French soldiers by force, and tried to be rid of our Acadian friends.

"For generations the Europeans used to come to to these shores just for the summer – Portugese, French, English. They would catch the fish, dry them in the sun, shoot a few geese and moose, then go home and leave us alone."

Sulian nodded. "These Scotchmen want to live on the land all year long – like the Acadians."

"Scots," corrected Mas'l.

"Many are friendly to us," said Sulian, ignoring the correction. "But just as many seem to be nervous.

"They don't understand the sacred bond between the people, the Life-giver and our Mother Earth."

"Our French friends grew gardens in fertile soil next to the rivers and left the rest to us." Mas'l paused. "But the English are giving away our hunting lands to these ones who come to our mountains, and they have to clear the land before they can support themselves. How bad must it be where they were to labour so?"

"For more than four generations, the Acadians have become a part of this land and our families," said Thomas. "They have learned to work with the land for their needs. The English want these ones, the wool-wearers, to break the land to their wants.

"I was told they didn't own the land on which they lived beyond the sunrise, and that their chiefs drove them off the land and onto ships. The English think they own our land and give it to these ones. Now they just want to be left alone."

"Tsk, they still don't own their land. How pitiful," clucked Eugene.

"That gives me an idea," said Sulian, conspiratorially. "We can't keep them out by force. They are learning from the earlier ones how to cope, but they really want to be left alone. Maybe we could make them feel uncomfortable, and they will leave on their own."

"Must be peaceful," Thomas cautioned. "Treaties."

"The English don't honour the treaties," Sulian reminded them, "but that is not my intention." He held up his hand to enumerate his reasoning. One – "they don't really want to mix." Two – "many are afraid of us and would rather be in their own homeland. If we get close to them..."

"Some would leave," interjected Eugene.

"You're catching on," said Sulian, dropping his hand. "Some would feel welcomed and more comfortable, but that's okay – at least they would fit in. But it might make many have second thoughts and leave."

"Good," said Mas'l. "Let's reach out. Help them. Make them feel welcome. What could go wrong?"

fin?

The Codcast
News and views from The Landing
Host: Tom E. Cod

Transcription services: Typecast Ink
No Internet? No Cellphone? No Problem!

[Begin]

Tom Cod **(TC):** Welcome to the Codcast.

In this episode we learn more about The
Landing's fastest growing enterprise – in
fact, the only growing enterprise that's
not actually growing, like in a garden.
They recently unveiled plans for yet another significant expansion.

Founded in 2012, Sterling's Self-storage
Services now has plans to not only en-
large the facility at its parent location
in The Landing, but they are also fielding
franchise enquiries. Apparently, there is
considerable interest.

In an interview at his summer residence,
his family's campground on Lake Ainslie,
entrepreneur Sterling Macaulay says his
company's dream of expansion has become

a reality, thanks in part to the Covid-19 pandemic.

Sterling Macaulay **(SM):** It sounds awful to say it, but being ordered to quarantine – the entire population of the campground was locked down for three days by the Lake Ainslie department of health (ed.) – was a godsend.

Sitting around the campfire with a few people and a few pops night after night, one's mind tends to wander. Or is that wonder? Like the time we decided to enter the self-storage space race. That's a joke.

TC: It's worth noting as background information – and to see how Macaulay's mind works – the genesis of Sterling's initial foray into the digital age of self storage. The company's first campus was the garage behind Sterling Macaulay senior's hardware store at the edge of the village.

SM: Minimalism is the new avarice. More and more, young people in particular desire fashionable tiny houses that just don't have room for the latest in desirable furnishings and conveniences. These days, our most prized possessions, things we can't do without, are things we can't afford.

Keeping pace with upsized tastes on pint-sized budgets is no easy feat. The skyrocketing cost of living includes the rising costs of contemporary housing causing, in turn, a social disconnect between desire and practicality. Media perpetuate

lifestyle images of unattainable excess –
an entire TV channel is devoted to home
renovations for families better suited to
auditioning for primetime soap operas.

TC: So, Sterling created Out-of-site
Solutions. Partnering with Amazon, the
world's leading online retailer, consumers can have it all without having it at
all! Macaulay explains.

SM: We feel it will become increasingly
important to ease people's guilt over
having too much without cramping their
aversion to having too little.

TC: Consumers in more prosperous locales
get caught in a dilemma – live large with
less.

SM: Our new motto addresses that: "Live
large and prosper." That's a play of words
– from *Star Trek*. Space is the final fron-
tier. Well, lack of it.

TC: Amazon's infamous Hot-pot 3.0, too big
for today's tiny-house kitchens, yet vital
to today's lifestyle, allows families to
display their prosperity without renovating to accommodate it. How, you ask?

SM: By avoiding the clutter resulting
from shopping. Purchases can be shipped
directly to the family storage unit, where
it would have ended up anyway.

TC: Immediately on purchase, Amazon will
email a digital image of the item – choice
of colours, etc. – direct to the buyer's
in-box while simultaneously shipping the
actual hot-pot to storage. Sterling's will

accept the acquired appliance for the family unit, and the buyer can trot out the picture of their appliance at will. The purchase can stay where it is (in storage) until the customer decides to re-gift, re-sell or forget about it.

As a bonus service, Sterling's continuously monitors Amazon for appliance updates using a proprietary program called ESP Home (extrasensory purchasing), using one of Amazon's latest patents: "always there" telepathic cloud connection. For example, a Sterling's client sees something online or in advertising, and ESP Home will not only sense the level of desire (variable by client choice), it will initiate the purchase and direct it to their storage unit – without anyone getting their hands dirty.

SM: Sterling's Self-storage serves mostly more prosperous populations in larger centres. But why should any family – whether in Port Hood, Port Hawkesbury, Port Credit or Port Alberni – stop buying just because they don't have all of the space that local bylaws allow. After all, when folks around here [i.e., The Landing] have too much, they store it on the front porch! Sterling's is good for the environment.

TC: What's next you ask? Meet Out-a-site, Out-a-mind.

With today's announcement, Sterling Macaulay says his company's self-storage dream enters an entirely new, but related, service – seniors storage. The company has announced it is expanding its storage campuses to include seniors' housing. Sterling's tiny granny flats will be specially designed residences for people's precious burden. Grandpa and grandma.

SM: Today's families are frustrated by the contradiction between concern for elders and concern for a clutter-free lifestyle.

Covid got us thinking inside the box, so to speak. We asked ourselves "What else can people no longer afford but can't bear to part with?"

Out-a-site, Out-a-mind Granny Flats take the guilt, frustration and smell out of elder care.

The pandemic restrictions on travel and traffic brought to light the age-old contradiction between concern for our elders, concern for ourselves and concern for living a clutter-free existence.

Our motto still needs work but it will be something along the lines of "Care for granny without the smell."

Bunny Gardner **(BG):** Seniors housing has become a real conundrum for the modern family.

TC: Bunny Gardner is vice-president in charge of Out-a-site.

In partnership with Budget Tiny Houses, seniors storage campuses capitalize on the tiny house movement.

BG: They're often confused anyway, so each granny flat's interior design can be coordinated with the family's primary dwelling, so their elders can feel included. No more guilt over the contradiction between concern for an elder and concern for appearances.

Think of it. Specially designed residences for your most precious burden. Each campus will consist of used sea cans arranged attractively to maximize available land. Not those full-size high-seas containers that take up so much room, just the pint-size versions. Big enough to hide you, small enough to keep you safe. Small boxes for small people.

TC: Here too, digital technology comes into play.

SM: Bunny and myself were sitting among friends around the campfire [at Bunny's place, overlooking the loch] saying how lucky we are to have all this great scenery – so relaxing. Lo and behold, our lightbulbs came on as bright as stars. We looked at each other wide-eyed. "Virtual," we said in unison.

TC: In a landmark deal between Sterling's, Canada Post and Google images and maps divisions, outsiders can now boast possession of prestigious loch-side addresses without having to "mortgage the farm," so-to-speak.

SM: Canada Post has signed with us a 99-year lease on 1,000 virtual P.O. boxes (VPOs) complete with postal codes. Then, with Google we have created a cross-referenced database of Google images of homes superimposed on loch-side views. Royalty-free, of course, because they're on Google!

BG: Pick a picture of a house, yard, even recreational vehicles. These can then be virtually associated with the digital address and postal code. Choose a house – click. Choose the colour – click. Choose the view – click. Choose a BBQ, a gazebo, an ATV – click, click, click.

SM: Ipso facto and you have pictures as proof of your Cape Breton home. No slow traffic getting in the way. No grass to mow, no bugs to swat, no tedious family trips on weekends. And no vandalism or break-and-enters!

TC: Macaulay adds that all this comes at a fraction of the cost of the real thing.

BG: Best of all, locals don't have to worry about heavy seasonal traffic and late-night partying. The virtual residents don't have to worry about break-and-enters, mice or racoons. There's nothing to break into and no contents to trash.

SM: Product testing scores equally well with seniors from immigrant families. Foreign pastoral scenes helped test-subjects to forget their dislike of the cold climate here and our puzzling array of by-laws like no smoking and speed limits. Neighbours (well, virtual neighbours) won't have to put up with those late-night phone calls on the front porch to distant relatives.

I forgot to mention, Sterling's proprietary digital fulfillment system can also connect directly with other shared services, like Uber Meals-on-wheels, and of course with Amazon. Granny's every wish can be attended to without coming too close.

TC: So, that's all pretty exciting. And to think it started right here in The Landing!

What's next for Stewart Macaulay and Sterling Self-storage? He's not saying, but – and remember that you heard it here first – we've heard from a reliable source that Macaulay's younger brother has a new camera and he's been seen taking pictures of people's pets at the campground.

Thanks for listening – or for reading.

Tune in next time when The Codcast meets Rachel, the hen made famous in Beatrice MacNeil's excellent novel, Where White Horses Gallop.

Until then, this is Tom E. Cod, for the Codcast.

fin

NOTES & INSPIRATIONS

"Finding Aonghas" (p. 1) was inspired by a remark overheard at the West Bay Road Fire Hall, and inspired by the role that a small town radio station plays in local news. A big thank you to the real 101.5 FM, "The Hawk" (Port Hawkesbury, NS) for letting me use their call sign. In fact, then-owner Bob MacEachern recorded fake news flashes for me so I could play them as part of a reading of the story to a local audience in 2018. Great fun!

"No Place Like Home" (p. 11) had a few inspirations, not the least of which are the village of West Bay Road, a family visit to Tancook Island, NS, and of course, Cape Breton's famous predelection for nicknames. A high school chum often joked that he was going to get a pet pig and name it Harmony. Hope he doesn't mind.

"Poor Woolly's Hallmark Christmas" (p. 55). Seeing countless Hallmark (TV) Channel movies in recent years, I have been struck by the fact that similar towns and villages seem to be used frequently, sometimes even back-to-back! I find myself looking for similarities and, of course, watching for stories set in places I've lived, places like Banff, AB. Many of the actors in the

Hallmark movies are familiar faces as well, especially stars from days gone by. I just love the idea of Poor Woolly meeting up with a TV idol on the set of a movie being shot in his home town.

Poor Woolly is partly inspired by observation of a young man in a large bookstore in Toronto. We have all seen such individuals, but I was struck by his engagement with the book he was reading, while standing, his periodic surveillance of the people around him as though relating them to what he was reading, and with the way he gently and rhythmically swayed back and forth as he read, perhaps to music in his head. He reminded me of an acquaintance, now deceased, from North Sydney, NS. David Wilkie, who was always around the racetrack (Standardbreds) in North Sydney, was brilliant, but very intense. His personality we today would characterize as somewhere on the autism spectrum.

An earlier version of "A Wing and a Prayer" (p. 85) won Ed's Books and More short fiction competition, Sydney, NS, 2018. The idea(s) incorporated into this story come from conversations about snow plows and drivers, over coffee with friends at the West Bay Road Fire Hall.

"Sandy Neal's Last Ride" (p. 92) is inspired by a storytelling session in Inverness, NS, celebrating the tall tales of Hector "Doink" MacDonald. The story of a highly skilled, if reckless, horse and wagon wrangler stuck with me.

For "A Man of Exceptionally Keen Discernment" (p. 110), many thanks to Barbara MacKay, West Bay, and Linda Campbell, Marble Mountain, for putting me onto the late Kenny McIntosh (1858-1947), who is a real person, and who was a real character by all accounts.

Apparently McIntosh had written articles in a newspaper about fireballs and marsh gases, and had corresponded with Albert Einstein. I have seen correspondence wherein McIntosh discusses (and argues with) Einstein's theories, but I haven't corroborated direct contact between them. So, I tinkered with Tesla, a fascinating character in his own right.

Marble Mountain had a huge limestone quarry. Some info on that was garnered locally, including a self-published book by Don Pillar titled *Out of the Limelight: A History of Marble Mountain, Cape Breton.*

The title for the story is a quote from "Procedings and Transactions of the Nova Scotia Institute of Science," 1906, Vol. XI, Part 2, Pp. 262-70, by Henry S. Poole. Mr. Poole presented McIntosh's paper on "The Question of Subsidence at Louisbourg, Cape Breton." It is Poole who referred to McIntosh as "a man of exceptionally keen discernment." How irresistible it that!

"The Codcast" (p. 159) was inspired by a conversation with my siblings, who casually observed the proliferation of self-storage businesses cropping up in places you'd not expect to generate so much "stuff" that so many people would need storage lockers. The lockers spoke to me as emblematic of our age of excess. The typography mimics that which you'd get with a transcription.

MIKE R. HUNTER is former Editor-in-Chief at Cape Breton University Press (retired). He has an MA in Communication and Culture from York and Ryerson (now Toronto Metropolitan) universities.

A native of Riverview, NB, Mike has lived all over Canada, but in Cape Breton since 1984. He's been associated with the university since 1996. He took over the press in 2003, guiding it from publishing four books annually to ten books annually by 2016.

Related employment experiences include managing editor of a small-town newspaper, freelance for the Halifax *Chronicle Herald* and other periodicals, as well as publication of a few articles in academic presses.

Some flash fiction stories have been long- and shortlisted for various prizes. The good folks at Tarbert Book Festival, Scotland, have shortlisted two flash fiction pieces. The original story "A Wing and a Prayer" won Ed's Books short fiction competition (Sydney, NS, 2018) and was subsequently published in the *Cape Breton Post*. Many other submissions have so far failed to make the grade – too bad for them – making this self-publication necessary (he needed to get these stories off his desk in order to move on).

Mike and families live in West Bay, Cape Breton, and in Toronto. He edits non-fiction books for others, and is working on a novel of his own. When not hunched over a manuscript, he may be found on the trails – hiking in summer, snowshoeing in winter – or having coffee and telling stories with the locals.